MIRACLE AT THE
HIGHER GROUNDS CAFÉ

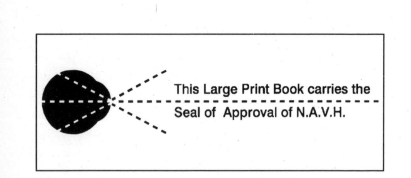

This Large Print Book carries the
Seal of Approval of N.A.V.H.

MIRACLE AT THE HIGHER GROUNDS CAFÉ

MAX LUCADO
WITH ERIC NEWMAN
AND CANDACE LEE

THORNDIKE PRESS
A part of Gale, Cengage Learning

Farmington Hills, Mich • San Francisco • New York • Waterville, Maine
Meriden, Conn • Mason, Ohio • Chicago

Copyright © 2015 by Max Lucado.
A Heavenly Novel.
Thorndike Press, a part of Gale, Cengage Learning.

LIBRARY OF CONGRESS CATALOGING-IN-PUBLICATION DATA

Lucado, Max.
  Miracle at the Higher Grounds Cafe / by Max Lucado with Eric Newman and Candace Lee.
    pages cm. — (A heavenly novel) (Thorndike Press large print Christian fiction)
  ISBN 978-1-4104-7644-9 (hardcover) — ISBN 1-4104-7644-8 (hardcover)
  1. Large type books. I. Title.
PS3562.U225M57 2015
813'.54—dc23
                                                    2014048847

Published in 2015 by arrangement with Thomas Nelson, Inc., a division of HarperCollins Christian Publishing, Inc.

Printed in Mexico
1 2 3 4 5 6 7 19 18 17 16 15

MIRACLE AT THE
HIGHER GROUNDS CAFÉ

CHAPTER 1

With one cup of coffee, Chelsea Chambers could rule the world. And by six a.m. she'd had several. Four, to be precise. The morning demanded it. Today was the grand reopening of her family's café. The quaint two-story structure had welcomed patrons in one of San Antonio's oldest neighborhoods, the King William District, for decades. As skyscrapers erupted a mile north and east, the neighborhood quietly maintained its distinctive old-world charm. Dormer windows. Pecan trees. Shingled houses with wooden porches. The homes sat in the shadows of bank buildings and hotels thirty stories tall.

Chelsea had grown up here. Her enterprising grandmother Sophia had converted the lower level of her Victorian home to a coffee shop just in time for the 1968 world's fair. The Confluence of Civilizations in the Americas was the fair's theme, and Sophia

Grayson had made good on its offer, flinging her doors wide open for coffee-loving patrons from around the world. Even Lady Bird Johnson paid a visit to the café, or so Grandmother Sophia had boasted. "The First Lady sat right on this very sofa, sipping cappuccino!"

Chelsea glanced at the floral Queen Anne sofa, still sitting in the corner after all these years. Every nook and cranny held a memory. When Sophia passed, Chelsea's mother, Virginia, took ownership of the café and its legacy of hospitality. Like Sophia before her, Virginia delighted in serving her guests a soothing cup of coffee, a slice of cake, and, when the occasion called for it, a prayer of encouragement.

And now it was Chelsea's turn. The plan was simple: occupy the twelve hundred square feet on the second floor and run the shop on the lower one. At least that was her mother's expectation when she willed the café to Chelsea. But times had changed. People were busier, coffee shops trendier. The antique lamps, sunken cushions, wooden floors, and delicate tea tables of the café were a far cry from the modern aesthetic of popular barista bars, but Chelsea hoped her patrons could appreciate the suggestion of simpler times.

8

The grandfather clock in the corner chimed six thirty, and Chelsea stopped to take one last look around the store. A chalkboard menu — painstakingly lettered — hung above the counter, and a glass-front case displayed the pride of her pantry: secret-recipe croissants and cupcakes. The blue swinging doors behind the counter concealed a gleaming kitchen. She should know — she'd wiped it down ten times that morning. There was nothing left to do.

Chelsea turned the lock and flipped the switch on the retro neon sign. "The Higher Grounds Café is officially open for business!" she announced.

The café's moniker echoed her grandmother's aspirations to see her customers leave with their spirits raised. Chelsea appreciated the lofty ideals. She only hoped she would live up to them.

"Isn't this exciting?" she asked her lone employee.

Tim nodded his head and fiddled with his handlebar mustache. The action hardly seemed sanitary, much less celebratory. Per résumé, Tim was the perfect employee. A recent graduate from the University of Texas, he had learned to pull a shot of espresso during a semester abroad in Rome. He spoke Italian and Spanish and claimed to be a morning person. Chelsea shuddered at the thought of what he might look like by noon.

"This is a historic moment!" she said, begging for a little enthusiasm.

Still nothing. Nothing but the pained expression Chelsea had come to know as Tim's face. Never mind. She was not about to let the faux lumberjack put a damper on her day.

Twelve-year-old Hancock bounded down the stairs wearing an oversized Dallas Cowboys jersey with *Chambers* emblazoned on the back. He surveyed the café. "What time do you open?"

"We are open," Chelsea said.

"So . . . where are all the people?" Hancock had a knack for making Chelsea feel self-conscious.

"They'll come," she said. "Where's your sister?"

Emily burst into the café just then, a six-year-old version of her mother. Except where Chelsea liked to blend in, Emily sparkled. Her glittery Mary Janes added to the effect. "Hancock helped me pick out my outfit," she boasted.

Chelsea took in her daughter's ensemble of sequins and stripes, and smiled. Yesterday's Chelsea would have made both children change before leaving the house. But today's Chelsea served her kids chocolate chip muffins and walked them to the bus stop, leaving a trail of glitter and crumbs.

"I hope you can manage the morning rush without me," Chelsea called to Tim.

Tim gave his boss a thumbs-up.

As the trio hurried down the front sidewalk, they felt the bite of cold air. The January sky was impossibly blue, but the temperature was surprisingly chilly.

"Let's zip up your jacket." Chelsea knelt to help Emily, venturing one more glance at the café front. Dormer windows protruded from the black-shingled roof. Vines crawled up a trellis on the side of the porch, where two worn wooden rockers sat side by side. A sidewalk bisected the neatly trimmed front lawn. Apart from the sign that hung from the porch, this could be someone's home.

Hard to believe it's my home again. So many memories.

But with each passing block of pristine Victorian mansions and refurbished Mission-style homes, the nostalgia began to wear thin. Everything Chelsea saw triggered a fresh idea, and by the time they reached the bus stop, her mental to-do list had grown:

buy new rockers for the porch
wash the windows
plant a garden
learn how to plant a garden

"You don't have to wait with us, you know," Hancock said as the yellow bus rounded the corner. "We've been doing this for two months now."

Chelsea looked at him, and for a moment saw his father in his face. High cheekbones and wide eyes bluer than a Texas sky, blond hair and small nose. *As long as he doesn't have his wild side,* she said to herself. "You're right. You two can walk back to the house on your own after school, okay?"

She turned her attention to Emily, who was bouncing with excitement. "Do you have your lunch box?"

"Si, madre," Emily said, giving her backpack a pat. Their new school had a Spanish immersion program, and Emily delighted in practicing her new words.

Chelsea gave her a big squeeze and then went to hug her son, but the look of dread in his eyes stopped her. She recalled a similar moment at the bus stop with her own mother.

"Hancock, I know we've been through a

lot lately. Thank you for trying to make it work."

As the bus pulled away, Chelsea inhaled deeply. This was a new thing for her. She could remember almost anything, but she had a bad habit of forgetting to breathe.

She rushed back to the café, arriving just in time for her first customer. Chelsea had met Bo Thompson only once, but at seventy years old and well over six feet tall, he was memorable. The gentlest of giants. Bo had been her mother's most faithful customer — one of the few remaining regulars of the Higher Grounds Café. "Best coffee in town," he insisted. It didn't hurt that he lived just across the street.

At the sight of Chelsea, Bo removed his baseball hat, revealing a shiny bald head. When they shook hands, his meaty palms swallowed Chelsea's.

"Big day for the neighborhood," his deep voice announced.

"Indeed it is." She smiled.

"Hope you don't mind the jersey, but my team won yesterday." He unzipped his jacket just enough to reveal the green and gold of the Green Bay Packers.

"You won't get any pushback from me," Chelsea said. "I don't really follow sports

13

these days. Now if I recall correctly, you go for a small cappuccino with extra foam?"

"I'm impressed," Bo said with a grin that filled his whole face.

Chelsea could feel Tim's critical eye as she worked. She might not have trained in Italy, but she knew how to make a cappuccino. Her mother had taught her to steam a pillow of foam so thick you could sleep on it. But as soon as that thought crossed her mind, the espresso machine began to sputter. Then it stopped.

Chelsea fiddled with the steam valve. "I don't . . . it's not . . ."

Tim plodded to Chelsea's aid. Out of the corner of her eye she caught Bo stealing a glance at his watch.

"How about a black coffee after all?" he said with a wink.

"One black coffee. On the house," Chelsea insisted with the promise of a cappuccino by morning.

"I'll miss seeing your mom every day, but it's good to see the shop open again," Bo said as Chelsea served him his drink. "Of course, it'd be even sweeter if you still had your mother's famous pumpkin cream cheese muffins."

Chelsea smiled. She was pleased to know the recipes she'd created for her mother were a hit. "Here. My gift to you." She bagged a freshly baked pumpkin muffin and handed it to Bo.

He found a dozen different ways to say thank you, then doubled back to tell Chelsea she had made his morning.

"You're not gonna make much money, giving stuff away," Tim said.

"Thanks for the tip, Tim," Chelsea said.

Chelsea could afford to sponsor as many free muffins as she liked. She had built up a treasury of mouth-watering recipes, and her sister, Sara, had been begging her to open up shop for years. But for Chelsea, the Higher Grounds Café wasn't really a business venture. It was a safe haven.

Ding! Ding! "Surprise!"

The slow morning had drifted into an even slower afternoon, and Chelsea lit up when she turned to see her sister standing in the doorway, holding a sunny bouquet of flowers.

"My house is spotless, and Tony has the twins for a few hours. So I'm here for your grand reopening."

There was an air of springtime about Sara. Everything about her radiated happiness. Her hair was long, straight, and golden as a sunrise. Her brown eyes sparkled and turned into half-moons when she laughed. Her smile lifted more on the right than the left because of the scar that stretched like a piano string from the corner of her mouth to her jaw.

"I thought you were showing your house today!" Chelsea said, succumbing to Sara's bear hug.

"Potential buyers cancelled. Again."

"Oh no! Well, when you do find a house, my offer still stands," Chelsea said. "I'm making the down payment. Maybe we'll end up neighbors after all!"

No one would ever peg the two as sisters. Sara was bubbly, Chelsea bookish. Sara was tall and blond; Chelsea, medium height and dark-haired like their mother. Sara had always had her pick of boyfriends. Chelsea, not so much. Still, they were best friends. Sara looked out for Chelsea. Chelsea looked up to Sara. For over a decade, the two had dreamed of living in the same city again.

"I still can't believe you're back in town!"

"Not exactly the way we wanted it to happen," Chelsea said.

"But you're here. And that's what matters, right?"

Chelsea marveled at her sister's optimism. More than once she'd wondered if Sara had been born with a double dose.

"You're right. Opening day is great. Great!" Chelsea tried mirroring Sara's rosy perspective. "Just getting the hang of things. It's fun being anonymous for a change, though a few more customers would be nice. 'Slow' doesn't do it justice."

Ding! Ding! The shopkeeper's bell announced an arrival. "You must be good luck!" Chelsea said.

Tim had been fiddling with the espresso machine since Chelsea's epic fail in front of Bo. Now he turned a nob, releasing a hiss of piping hot steam from the espresso machine. "And we're back," he said with satisfaction.

And not a moment too soon. A surprising rush of customers had filled the shop. Chelsea put on her warmest smile. "Welcome to Higher Grounds. What can I get y'all?"

"We heard you had some autographed football stuff from the Dallas Cowboys," said the group's ringleader. His towering size and lettered jacket pegged him as a high school football star.

"I wouldn't know anything about that," Chelsea said. "But our customers say we have the best coffee in town."

"Customers?" Tim mumbled behind Chelsea's back. She knew it was a stretch.

17

"But you're her, right?" asked a prom queen with a Café Cosmos coffee tumbler. "The wife of that football guy."

Chelsea struggled for words. "I am . . ."

Sara swooped in for the rescue. "She's the owner of this café."

"So is Sawyer Chambers your husband or not?"

A simple yes or no might do the trick. But to Chelsea it was more complex. More layered. There were nuance and history to consider. Lots of history.

"Some kid in my little brother's class said so." The quarterback turned for confirmation to a middle school version of himself. "Right?"

Ding! Ding! Hancock and Emily entered the café.

"Yeah! *He* was telling people at school." The middle schooler outed Hancock, who stopped dead in his tracks.

Hancock knew he was in trouble but did his best to play it cool in front of the older students. "Hey, man . . . I, uh, better go start on my homework," he said to his classmate. "See ya tomorrow."

Chelsea eyed her son as he made his escape. "I was just trying to get you some customers," he mumbled on the way up the stairs.

Emily had spotted her Aunt Sara and run to her for a hug.

A boy with a smartphone held it up for all to see. "That's her all right. Look. Mrs. Sawyer Chambers."

Mrs. Chambers. There it was, plain and simple. Practically Amish.

"You're kinda famous," the boy said.

If a picture could tell a thousand words, then a Google image search could tell ten thousand. Swipe, swipe, swipe. Chelsea's life flashed before her eyes — and everyone else's, for that matter. The room was getting smaller, the smartphone screen bigger. Until finally . . .

"Who's that?" said the young magician who had turned his smartphone into an IMAX screen. The image stretched as far as the east is from the west: Sawyer Chambers in the arms of another woman. A redheaded beauty. A triple threat — younger, thinner, and prettier.

The leader of the pack looked at the picture and then at the woman behind the counter and stated the obvious. "That's not you."

"OMG," said the prom queen with a look of pity.

All eyes shifted to Chelsea. "Can I interest y'all in a cupcake?" she managed through gritted teeth.

The prom queen broke the silence. "I'll take one," she said, motioning for her friends to flee the awkward scene. "To go."

As the café emptied, Chelsea melted into the counter, defeated. "Life was so much simpler before the Internet," she moaned.

"Don't you waste another minute worrying about the Internet," Sara said, wrapping her in a hug.

"You're right," Chelsea said, pulling herself together. "I'm sure it'll never take off."

CHAPTER 2

Samuel watched from a distance. From heaven's view, things were simpler. Clearer. Unobstructed by the clamor of everyday life. He peered through the stars, assessing the once familiar landscape.

What he saw stirred concern. He remembered his first assignment here. The region had a sparkle to it, a glow. Now a pall had settled on the city. Entire neighborhoods were hidden by shadows.

But still there were beacons of light. Like spires alit with gold, they punctured the darkness, streaking past Samuel and into the heavens.

It's dusk, Samuel thought, *but not night. Not yet.*

He took note of an embedded glow and set his eyes on the source. The corner of the Higher Grounds Café. This place had been prayed for and prayed over.

The Father won't relinquish this territory eas-

21

ily, not without a fight. And I love a good fight!

Prayers move God. And God moves angels. So Samuel was being sent. Other angels had more experience. Other angels had more strength. But no angel in heaven could match Samuel's resolve. This was his first solo mission.

"Sammy," he said to himself, "time to fly."

He grasped the hilt of his fiery saber and lifted his small frame to its full height. He tightened his muscles, squinted his eyes, leaned forward, and speared earthward. The wind rushed his hair straight back. As he broke through the clouds, he spotted the figure of Chelsea sitting on her porch and wondered what role she was going to play in this unfolding saga. He was, after all, her guardian angel.

CHAPTER 3

It was a Friday night, and Chelsea was baking. She hummed as she worked. After years of feeling the pressure to keep up with the trophy wives of the ripped and famous, she welcomed the change of pace. Not to mention the boost in confidence. Her run-in with the posse of high schoolers had been redeemed (well, almost) when the prom queen called back to order five dozen of "those delicious cupcakes" for her mom's birthday tea. It was the perfect opportunity for Chelsea to reintroduce herself to the community. She had dreamed up a grand entrance — a light, lemon cake topped with a swirl of Earl Grey–infused buttercream frosting.

Baking was therapy for Chelsea, and she was ready for a nice, long session. The complexity of her recipes had a funny way of matching the complexity of her problems. The day she learned of Sawyer's infidelity, she baked a thirteen-layer bittersweet choco-late cake — one for each year they were married. After one bite, she dropped the entire thing in the trash. She remembered the acrid aftertaste like it was yesterday. She did a quick calculation. Eight months and seventeen days ago, exactly.

"Time will heal all wounds," Chelsea's mother said.

And she would know. *Forgive and forget* were words Virginia Hancock had lived by, but Chelsea wasn't so sure. Forgetting was not in her nature. Especially when it came to Sawyer.

Sawyer was drafted into the NFL less than a year after he and Chelsea were married. He spent eight seasons with the Cowboys, during which he played like an all-star and aged like a rock star. Led the league in rush-ing for three seasons. The Cowboys reached the play-offs twice. Sawyer was a regular ESPN highlight. People were already talk-ing Hall of Fame. But a knee-level tackle in the first game of his ninth season finished that. Torn ACL.

Sawyer had signed a fifteen-million-dollar contract, guaranteed healthy or not. He could have retired. He *should* have retired. Instead, determined to make a comeback, he rehabbed his leg and earned a spot with the Seattle Seahawks. But he was not the same player. And he knew it.

Many a pro athlete goes through a midlife crisis. For Sawyer, it happened at the ripe old age of thirty-five. After three rough seasons in Seattle, he was third string. He overcompensated for his failures on the field with risky business ventures, extravagant gestures, and late nights on the town. Chelsea tried to shield her kids from their father's sudden change in behavior, but she couldn't keep up. Sawyer couldn't settle down.

By the start of the next season, the Seahawks dropped him. So did his agent. No one was interested in Sawyer anymore. No one except for Cassie Lockhart, a junior agent who was young and hungry and eager to represent an NFL star. She convinced Sawyer to join her for a meeting with the San Diego Chargers. Chelsea guessed she was after the commission. She had no idea the girl was after her husband.

"It was the biggest mistake of my life," Sawyer pleaded.

"It's certainly one for the record books," Chelsea deflected. "Not to mention the tabloids and social media."

A few months later Chelsea left Seattle. And Sawyer. That's when Sawyer vowed he would change.

I wonder how that's going for him.

Chelsea had not spoken to Sawyer since. Her mother's untimely death provided the perfect opportunity to start over. Or at least escape. She imposed strict communication rules when she moved back to her old hometown.

"Half an hour with the kids each day?" he asked.

"Yes, but they call you," she negotiated.

He agreed to her terms as long as she agreed this was only a "trial separation." The jury was still out. Chelsea had divorced Sawyer a dozen times in her imagination, but she had two reasons that kept her from going through with it, and they were sleeping upstairs. Hancock and Emily loved their dad in spite of all his flaws.

"Wish I could do the same," Chelsea said aloud, as she boxed the last of the cupcakes. The first special order of the Higher Grounds Café was complete. She paused to admire her handiwork. *Perfect.* And they needed to be. Tomorrow she would deliver them to one of San Antonio's most prestigious neighborhoods. And if she was going to make it on her own, without Sawyer, her new life had to start now.

■ ■ ■ ■

From Chelsea's café, Alamo Heights was due north, both on the map and in social standing. Chelsea's SUV weaved up a hill lined with flawless homes and inviting gardens, typical of the coveted 09 zip code.

"I miss our old house," Hancock said as they arrived at the delivery address.

Chelsea glanced up at a pristine Tudor home. It held an uncanny resemblance to their house in Seattle. Whoever lived here did not need the ten-dollar gift certificate she planned to deliver with the cupcakes. But after a slow week, Chelsea was feeling the need to re-establish the Higher Grounds Café in the community.

Hancock rattled on. "I miss living by the water. Having my own room. Our backyard. The game room. Dad's giant TV . . ."

"Okay, mister!" Chelsea interrupted. "We'll find a new house before long. Something nice. In the meantime, start thinking of some things you're grateful for." She reached her right hand over and knuckle-rubbed her son's hair. "For example, I'm grateful for some one-on-one time with you."

She hoped the feeling was mutual. Chelsea

had, after all, rescued Hancock from an afternoon of tea parties with his little sister and the babysitter.

Chelsea stacked several boxes of cupcakes into Hancock's open arms, and together they walked toward the grandiose front door.

Chelsea rang the doorbell and waited, imagining lighthearted table talk and celebratory clinking of champagne glasses within. It was strange to be on the outside, but the soirees and black-tie benefits — those were Sawyer's thing. He was the life of the party, and she often got lost in the shuffle. But not today. Chelsea relished the simplicity of her assignment. For a brief moment, she even contemplated introducing herself by her maiden name.

She didn't get to make a decision. The door opened to a slender blond woman who could have stepped off a catalog page showcasing "casual elegance." She wore a diamond pendant above her asymmetrical black top, a black-and-white viscose skirt that seemed to float about her, and a surprised expression. "Chelsea Chambers?"

"Deb Kingsly?"

Deb threw her arms around Chelsea. "It feels like a million years!" she said. "I haven't seen you since . . ."

Chelsea knew exactly when. "The wedding," she said, almost whispering.

"Right," Deb said, glancing at Hancock. "And who is this handsome fellow?"

"This is Hancock — my delivery guy," Chelsea quipped. "I reopened Mom's café this week, and . . . I hope I'm not ruining a surprise, but I think your daughter ordered birthday cupcakes."

"And she's been raving about them all week. I can't believe you're back! Come help me put the cupcakes on a platter, and then I have to introduce you to everyone." Deb dragged Chelsea and Hancock into the kitchen, and from there to the formal living room. A dozen women, all well-dressed, some cosmetically curved, formed a horseshoe around Chelsea, who wore jeans, a sweatshirt, and tennis shoes.

"Everyone, this is my childhood friend, Chelsea Chambers, wife of Sawyer Chambers." Deb paused for the gasps. "She just moved back to San Antonio to reopen the old Higher Grounds Café in King William. Y'all have to stop by and make her feel welcome!"

Chelsea smiled, grateful for Deb's thoughtful (and very Texan) introduction. Each woman introduced herself and promised to visit the store. Most importantly, the cupcakes were a big hit. More than one diet was momentarily abandoned.

Chelsea took the long route back, scouting out potential homes along the way. Somewhere, nestled among the pecan trees and terra cotta roofs, was the steeple of Alamo Heights Methodist, the church where she and Sawyer were married. On the surface it was a storybook wedding: The red carpet and white pews. Flowers everywhere. Each member of the Longhorn backfield dressed in a tux. Her sister and two best friends as bridesmaids. Her mother in the front row. But the bride walked down the aisle alone, carrying white roses and a child in her womb.

"So does this mean we're staying in San Antonio for good?" Hancock asked as Chelsea stopped to pluck a real estate brochure from beneath the For Sale sign of a picture-perfect home.

"Would that be so bad?" Chelsea asked.

"Maybe not. Not if Dad was with us."

As Chelsea passed from one zip code to the next, she noticed that yet another Café Cosmos had sprouted. A *Now Hiring* banner hung beneath the slick sign, but business was already booming. Luxury cars wrapped around the drive-through lane. Patrons spilled onto the patio, where the sunshine had convinced everyone it was spring.

When Chelsea got back to the café, she was pleased to see a customer. But he hadn't come for the coffee.

"Can you sign for the Higher Grounds Café?" the uniformed postal carrier asked.

"I am the owner," Chelsea offered with confidence. Her burst of esteem was but a vapor. The letter was from the IRS.

Chapter 4

"Eighty-six thousand dollars?" Sara exclaimed so loudly Chelsea had to hold the phone at arm's length.

"And seventy-eight cents," Chelsea added. "Did you know about this?"

"No, of course not. I mean . . . did Mom even know about this?"

"According to the notice, they hand-delivered three letters. And she signed for each one."

"I'm so sorry, Chelsea. I wish I could help. The church pays us a salary, but it's modest."

"Please don't worry about it. I can take care of the debt. Mom knew that."

Sara sighed. "Well, it makes sense why she left you the café. Now I feel guilty about getting all of Grandma's jewelry!"

"And all this time I thought I was her favorite," Chelsea deadpanned.

"So I guess this would be a bad time to

tell you that you were adopted?"

Sara could always make Chelsea laugh, even when her stomach was in knots. "Nothing would surprise me these days."

"Famous last words, sis."

The terms were as simple as they were strict. Pay $86,000.78 within thirty days, or the IRS would seize and sell all the assets of the Higher Grounds Café. Unfortunately, Chelsea and the kids were living in the only asset worth seizing. She needed to pay. Which meant she needed to speak with Sawyer.

That evening Chelsea tucked the kids into bed, tidied up the kitchen, and folded the laundry. When she couldn't put it off any longer, she went to her nightstand for her phone. It wasn't where she had left it, and she thought of taking that as a sign to save the call for another day. But it wasn't like her to lose things.

Chelsea scoured the café, pulled apart the sofa, and even looked in the washing machine. No phone. She was walking down the hall in defeat when a muffled laugh escaped the kids' bedroom.

She cracked open the door and saw a bluish glow escaping from under the covers of the top bunk.

"The guy was seven feet off the ground! I wish you could've been there." Hancock's whisper swelled with excitement.

"Me too," came a familiar voice on the other end of the line.

Chelsea drew a nice, long breath and approached the bed.

"All right, chatterbox," she said softly. The figure beneath the sheets froze. The voice on the other end of the line fell silent, and a sheepish Hancock emerged.

"I know I shoulda asked . . ." Hancock started to explain, his voice growing louder.

Chelsea put a finger to her to lips and extended her hand.

Hancock returned the iPhone to its rightful owner, sneaking a peek at the bunk below. To his relief, Emily was still sound asleep.

"Good night, Hancock." Chelsea gave him a warning look and crept out of the room. She pocketed the phone and started down the hall.

"Uh . . . Chelsea?"

She jumped. A hearty chuckle was now coming from her back pocket.

Chelsea pulled out her phone. Sawyer's face filled the screen.

"That's what I was hoping to see," Sawyer said. "Not that I don't admire the other view," he added, flashing Chelsea a mischievous smile with ivory white teeth.

She flipped over the phone, leaving Sawyer with a lovely panorama of her grandmother's oriental rug. She knew better than to FaceTime with Sawyer Chambers. Chelsea smoothed her ponytail, exhaled through gritted teeth, then turned over the phone to face him. Briefly.

"I need to speak with you," she told him. "Can I call you back?"

Twenty minutes later, Chelsea's blood was boiling. "Why am I just finding out about this?" she shouted into the phone.

"You wouldn't take my calls!" Sawyer countered. "What'd you want me to do? Send a singing telegram? A bouquet of flowers?"

And with that Chelsea hung up.

Fifteen million dollars would last most people a lifetime. Not Sawyer Chambers. He had invested in oil fields, commercial real estate, and junk bonds. He speculated in Miami condos and Arizona windmills. He could have more easily held a greased pig than his money. Nothing worked.

Chelsea had known the money was going fast, but she had a safety net. Four million dollars in an annuity fund that Sawyer had promised he would not touch. Not without talking to her first.

Another broken promise. Sawyer had sunk his last million into a franchise at Dallas Love Field. Within six months the creditors were at his door, and he'd had no choice but to drain the account. "It was that or bankruptcy," he had reasoned.

Chelsea could picture the face that went with that pleading tone. Furrowed brow, square jaw, to-die-for blue eyes. She knew all Sawyer's looks by heart. Thirteen years ago, that same famous face had persuaded Chelsea to skip her psychology class and go two-stepping at Sandy Springs Dance Hall . . .

Sawyer's image adorned the cover of the football program their junior year at the University of Texas. The photo caught him midair in a goal-line nosedive over his offensive line. Yes, he scored. In that game and twenty-two consecutive others. Everyone knew Sawyer Chambers.

No one knew Chelsea Hancock. She was the shy, studious type, wide-eyed at the sight of a campus of thirty-five hundred students. The school was ten times larger than the high school she attended. If not for her academic scholarship, she would have gone home after the first semester. Her grades were stellar, but her social life? She was queen of the library. She nearly dropped the phone when Sawyer Chambers called. He had seen her tutoring ad for the summer session on a bulletin board in the library. Her study-abroad fund needed a boost. As did his GPA.

"So you're the girl who's going to help me stay eligible for the Heisman," Sawyer said the first time they met.

"The Heimlich?"

"No," he chuckled, "the Heisman. As in the trophy for the best collegiate football player."

She gave him a blank look.

He struck a half back posture, cradling an invisible football and stiff-arming an invisible tackler. Still no response.

"You've never heard of it, have you?"

Chelsea had blushed, then recovered. "No, but I have heard of Hemingway. Have you?"

And so the relationship began.

By their fourth meeting she noticed Sawyer studying more than books.

"What? I like looking at you," he defended when she told him to focus. "Other girls flaunt and flirt. You don't have to. You're sneaky pretty."

Her face reddened. "And you're pretty

sneaky. Pay attention, Sawyer."

A week later they went on their first date.

"I need a girl like you. You think for yourself," Sawyer told her as he walked her to the door. "You always have the right answer."

Chelsea was skeptical. *Why would he notice me?* she wondered as she studied her just-dressed self in the full-length mirror. Her figure was slender, too shapeless for her taste. Chelsea could think of a dozen girls who were better suited for the Big Man on Campus.

But the first time they danced she knew they had something special.

Chelsea would never forget the look on Sawyer's face when he spun her into his arms. The intense gaze, the crooked smile. No one had ever looked at her that way before. "Is it too soon to say I love you?" he had asked. She felt like they were the only two people in the room. And she never wanted that feeling to go away.

Chelsea was pregnant by the end of the summer. Unable to come up with a solution she could live with, she confided in Sawyer. And for once he was the one with the answers. "Marry me," he said. "We can do this. We can make this work. Together."

Together. Had she known the pain *together*

would bring, would she have said yes?

Chelsea eased herself into the rocking chair on the porch. She needed a moment to clear her mind. She sipped from a steaming mug and pulled her mother's quilt tight around her shoulders. She and her mom had spent many nights in this very spot, gazing at the heavens. "You're loved, Chelsea. It's written in the stars," she would say.

But the stars weren't shining tonight.

Chelsea was broke. The air was cold. Her heart even colder. She had to divorce Sawyer. She had to make this work on her own.

CHAPTER 5

Watching and waiting. It seemed like all he ever did these days. And Samuel longed for more.

A heavy cloud had begun to encircle Chelsea. Clouding her judgment. Darkening her thoughts. The enemy had set its trap. And Chelsea was walking blindly forward.

If only she would ask for help. A simple prayer. Even a hint. God takes hints.

Samuel might have been a guardian angel, but he had a warrior's heart. If heaven had a playbook, Samuel knew it backward and forward. Messengers, warriors, guardians. He knew the greats by name and their moves by heart. And now he had an idea. A bold one. But he could not act without permission.

Watching and waiting.

Something in the distance caught Samuel's eye. A glimmer of light. Like a shooting star, a heavenly messenger was fast approaching.

"Gabriel!" Samuel stood at attention, stretching his frame. Even on his tiptoes, he only reached Gabriel's shoulder.

"You can relax, Samuel," Gabriel said, with a nod of approval.

"Have you reviewed my plan?"

"It's been making the rounds." Gabriel's expression gave nothing away.

"I know it's a little ambitious. Unconventional even." Samuel's nervous chatter grew faster with each word. "But there's precedent. We've set up this kind of gateway on earth before. This is just a new take. Like Jacob's Ladder 2.0!"

Gabriel placed a hand on Samuel's shoulder to calm him. "There's a lot of potential, Samuel. But the plan's a bit premature."

"I see." Samuel's shoulders sank. *More waiting.*

"Don't be discouraged," Gabriel said. "Heaven, it seems, has other plans."

Samuel's ears perked. "Like what?" He grabbed the hilt of his sword, eager for action.

Gabriel gave a knowing smile. "For this assignment, you don't need a sword."

CHAPTER 6

"Mom! It's burning!" Emily's voice carried downstairs to the café.

"Don't touch anything, I'm coming!" Chelsea had just finished updating the chalkboard menu with today's special: Million-Dollar Pie.

"Mom!"

Chelsea raced up the stairs, glancing at her phone. Still no response from Tim.

"What's burning, sweetheart?"

Emily stood on a chair in a cloud of smoke. "My toast!"

"Hancock!" Chelsea called. "Could you monitor your sister? And her breakfast?"

Hancock grumbled.

Ding! Ding! Customers. Where was Tim? It was seven a.m., and Chelsea had already sent him three texts. One more wouldn't hurt.

WHERE R U?!

Now back to the kids. "Why don't you

guys finish getting dressed? I'll have breakfast ready for you in the café."

Ding! Ding! Chelsea raced downstairs to take on her first bona fide morning rush.

"Well, isn't this a pleasant surprise!"

Chelsea's old friend Deb was standing at the counter alongside three other 09ers of Alamo Heights. All were decked out in their version of casual: slim designer jeans and leather jackets.

"This place hasn't changed a bit!" Deb drank in the familiar sights and sounds. "Brings back so many memories!"

Chelsea and Deb reminisced as she made the women their skinny vanilla lattes. Once Deb and her posse were tucked away in a cozy corner, Chelsea improvised a quick breakfast for the kids. She was just zipping up Emily's jacket when her phone buzzed with a message from Tim. *Finally,* she thought. Then she read his response.

TOOK A JOB AT CAFÉ COSMOS. THEY OFFER BENEFITS AND STUFF. SORRY. TRIED TO TELL U YESTERDAY BUT U LOOKED KINDA BUSY. ;-)

"You've got to be kidding me," Chelsea muttered, searching for an emoticon that matched the look on her face. But a fire-spewing dragon figure did not exist.

"What's wrong, Mommy?" Emily asked.

43

"You look really mad."

"It's Dad, isn't it?" Hancock guessed.

"No, no. It's fine. Everything's fine." She attempted a smile.

Ding! Ding! "Morning, Bo!" Emily said.

Bo Thompson had become a highlight of the kids' morning routine. He was warm and neighborly — even before his first cappuccino of the day. He seemed to wake up that way.

"I'll be right with you, Bo." Chelsea handed the kids their lunch money. "Are you okay walking your sister to the bus stop this morning?" she asked Hancock. "Mom's a little short on help today."

"I'd be happy to walk with them," Bo offered. "I'm heading in that direction."

Ding! Ding! Two more customers entered the café.

"You're a godsend, Bo," Chelsea said with a sigh of relief. "And your cappuccino's on the house today."

"Don't worry about it. We all need help every now and then."

It was true. Chelsea needed help. Now. And then she needed eighty-six thousand dollars. But first things first.

During a welcome lull, she posted a help-wanted ad on Craigslist. Her last attempt had produced Tim, so this time she got

44

specific: *Ideal candidate is personable and punctual with a positive attitude. Must love kids, coffee, and cupcakes.*

Within minutes of her posting the ad, her ideal candidate walked right through her front door. At least, that's what he tried to do.

"Are you okay?" Chelsea ran outside to help the stunned man to his feet.

"That has to be the cleanest glass in all of Texas," he exclaimed with a cheery Latino accent. "And you can tell the owner I said that."

"You just did," Chelsea replied. The man's bright demeanor brought a smile to her face. "Come on in. I'll get you something to drink."

Something about him captured Chelsea's attention. It wasn't just the black leather cowboy boots adorned with turquoise stones, nor the bright green pants, nor the floral Hawaiian shirt, nor even the Seattle Seahawks cap. She studied him for a moment: medium height, square frame, round face. *I know you from somewhere.* But for once her memory seemed to be failing her.

"I'm sorry, have we met?" she asked.

"Many people ask that question, *señora*. I must have a familiar face."

Manuel, or Manny, as he liked to be

called, wanted to chat. He had finally been granted citizenship at the age of thirty. Originally from Mexico, he was single and had moved to San Antonio to be near family.

"Have you already found a place to live?" Chelsea asked as she prepared his drink of choice: a vanilla latte with a generous helping of whipped cream.

"Yes. I have sisters in town. I'm staying with them until I find a steady job."

"What kind of work are you looking for?"

Before Manny could answer, a sudden burst of steam escaped the malfunctioning espresso machine. Frothy milk splattered across the countertop and onto Chelsea's apron.

"That machine was *supposed* to have been fixed!" she exclaimed. "Will you excuse me?" She disappeared into the adjoining kitchen in search of a fresh apron.

When she returned, Manny was standing behind the now spotless counter, tinkering with the espresso machine. "I hope you don't mind me taking a look," he said.

Chelsea eyed the cash register. *Untouched.*

"Go ahead. Try it now," he said, stepping aside.

Chelsea approached the machine with caution. She placed a fresh pitcher beneath

46

the steamer and turned the dial. Three perfect bursts of steam. Chelsea was impressed. "What is it you said you do?"

The staff of the Higher Grounds Café doubled that afternoon. Of course, the dress code took a little negotiating.

"Manny, you'll have to lose that hat. We're not Seahawks fans. And let's stick with solid colors from now on."

That night Chelsea ticked *Find help* off her mental to-dos. If only her other problems were that easy to solve. She was already dreading the next item on her list: *Negotiate terms of payment with the IRS.*

CHAPTER 7

Chelsea was a whiz at math. Sawyer used to joke that solving math puzzles gave her the kind of buzz he got from a good workout. But today math was just giving her a headache.

With the help of Sawyer's old accountant, she had managed to negotiate the tax debt to nine easy payments of $9,555.64. Easy, as long as she sold 155 lattes a day. A mere 500 percent increase of her daily business. Chelsea was doomed.

She was doomed the moment she married Sawyer, and after a few Google searches she had the numbers to prove it: 78 percent of former NFL players file for bankruptcy, and 50 percent of their marriages end in divorce. And with these stress-inducing statistics, Chelsea would be baking her way to the 69 percent of Americans who are overweight.

"You look like a cupcake."

Those are the words Chelsea heard. "Excuse me?"

"I said, you look like you could use a cupcake," Manny offered. Cautiously.

"Oh . . . um. Not today. But I could use a shot of espresso. Thanks, Manny."

In just over a week Manny had more than proven his worth. He was an early riser with a knack for being there right when Chelsea needed him. He was remarkable with her customers and even better with her kids. But for all his skill and intuition, Chelsea had never come across a more uncoordinated person — fashionably or physically. He couldn't master the swinging doors to the kitchen. The first few times, he would open one like it was a traditional door. When it would swing back, he would open it again.

"Manny," Chelsea finally had to tell him, "it won't stay open. Just walk right through it." He did, but stopped so soon the closing door popped him in the back. "Manny, you have to keep walking."

"Yes, ma'am."

"Haven't you seen one of these before?"

"Hmm, I don't think so."

He couldn't seem to keep his legs under him, which became a running joke in the café. "I make more friends falling over than most people do standing up," Manny would say. In fact, that was how Manny bonded with Sara.

"I have an idea!" Sara had backed into the café on a Wednesday morning, pulling her four-month-old sleeping twins in a double stroller. "Several, actually. But first, an Americano. Double shot. No, make it a triple. I haven't slept all week."

Chelsea had to admit her sister looked more frazzled than usual.

Sara rattled on. "The real estate agent ordered us out of the house for the next six hours. We have three second showings today!"

"That sounds promising! Are you and Tony still planning to make an offer on that house on Sierra? It looks perfect for you!"

"No." Sara hesitated, carefully formulating a sunny response. "It's a great neighborhood, but we decided it was a bit too much house for us right now." Her tone betrayed a hint of disappointment that hit Chelsea with a pang of guilt. Sara had called that Victorian cottage their dream home, and Chelsea knew her promised down payment would have made their dream a reality.

So much for playing the fairy godmother. I can't even make my own dreams come true.

"Are you sure you should be having all

that caffeine?" Chelsea asked, as Sara pushed her stroller up to the counter.

"I just need to hold it. And smell it. Is that so bad?"

"How 'bout a quad?"

"I love you."

"Hey, Manny?" Chelsea called back to the kitchen. Manny emerged wearing a bright orange shirt and an even brighter smile. He looked not unlike a traffic cone.

"You must be the sister! So pleased to meet you," he said, reaching across the counter to shake her hand. "I visited your church on Sunday."

Sara's face brightened with recognition. "I know you. You're the domino guy!"

Manny beamed, nodding like a bobble-head.

"Well, I hope we see you again," Sara continued. "Maybe next time, you can bring her along," she added, giving Chelsea a playful glance.

"I promise not to knock her over!" The two dissolved into laughter.

"Okay, people, fill me in. What's a domino guy?"

After a few false starts and lots of giggling, Chelsea got the story.

"So we're all lining up for Communion, and Shirley Benson is moving down the aisle at a snail's pace. She's such a dear, but seriously, Chelsea. Possibly the slowest moving human being on earth. Then out of nowhere, Manny here . . ."

"I tripped on Miss Shirley's cane and fell right to the ground. Then Miss Shirley went down. And so on, and so on."

"Six people, Chelsea. Like dominoes!" Sara said, growing serious. "It's a miracle no one was hurt." Then they all burst out laughing again.

"Wait a second! Shirley Benson dropped in yesterday, no pun intended, and I'd say she was downright spry," Chelsea said, turning to Manny. "She walked right up to the counter and gave you a big tip, if I remember correctly."

"Maybe you helped her out after all!" Sara added with a laugh.

Chelsea smiled. In spite of recent events, moments like these made her happy to be back home. Near family.

"Well?" she asked, taking a seat across from Sara, who was now inhaling the aroma of her steamy mug of espresso.

"It's perfection. I'm just going to take one sip," she whispered. "Don't tell the babies."

Chelsea laughed. "C'mon! I want to hear your idea!"

"Of course." Sara finished her sip. "I was

thinking . . . we need to create some buzz in the community!"

"That's it? That's the big idea?"

"Well . . . I was thinking of calling the *Tribune.* They could do an article on the grand reopening. Also, Tony's been wanting to add a little café at our church. We've got the space for it. And it'd be more exposure for you."

"Sure. I could do the church thing," Chelsea offered.

"And the *Trib*?" Sara knew she was venturing into tricky waters.

"That's a pass for me," Chelsea said. "I don't need any favors from Dad. Or his old cronies."

"C'mon. Dad hasn't worked at the *Tribune* for years!" Sara rolled her eyes. "Besides, things are different now."

"That's great, but I don't really need to hear about him. He didn't want to be a part of my life. And, well, it seems to be working out. Let's move on. Next idea."

"Well, we can't move on." Sara paused, then let it all out. "Please don't be mad, but I already called. They're sending someone tomorrow to interview you."

"Sara!"

"You need this, Chelsea. And it'll be great. I know it."

Chelsea wanted to give Sara an earful and walk away. But she was struck with a chilling truth. Sara was all she had left. Without her sister, she really was on her own. Chelsea could not afford any more grudges, so instead she forced a smile.

"Well, Manny," Chelsea called to her star employee, "let's get this café ready for the press!"

CHAPTER 8

The reporter was due to arrive the next day just in time for the morning rush. At least, Chelsea hoped there'd be a rush. An interview in an empty café would make for a pitiful story. Like only one guest coming to your birthday party kind of pitiful. But Chelsea couldn't think about that now. She had a job to do.

And she had just the right tools for this job: her cupcake recipes, all laid out on the café counter, each designed with a specific purpose in mind. Chocolate-covered raspberry (romantic), gingerbread (cozy), bananas Foster (luxurious), white chocolate mousse (elegant), dark chocolate truffle (decadent), birthday cake (festive) . . . This was a difficult decision.

"Mom?"

Chelsea turned to see little Emily in her pajamas, clutching a storybook. "Are you gonna tuck me in?"

Chelsea glanced at the oven. She had some time before the next batch would need to be ready. "Manny?"

Manny slammed into and then through the swinging doors of the kitchen.

"Would you keep an eye on the oven for me? I have a date with a very important person," she said.

Emily beamed.

"*Si, señora.*"

"*Hasta mañana,* Manny!" Emily called as she skipped out of the kitchen. "That's Spanish, Mom. It means see you tomorrow."

Tomorrow. Oh. My. Gosh. It's tomorrow!

Chelsea awoke with a start and glanced at the clown clock on the wall. Six thirty! She was late and trapped. Stuck between a soundly sleeping Emily and a wall.

"All right, everyone. Up!" Chelsea chucked the storybook she'd fallen asleep reading and shimmied out of the lower bunk. "C'mon, kiddos. Rise and shine. And do it fast. It's time to open the café!"

Chelsea charged Hancock with getting his sister ready for school and raced down the stairs, smoothing her wild halo of frizz.

Her mind was racing with the list of things she needed to do. So much so, she barely noticed the gleaming floors or strawberry cupcakes in her display. Then she took in the scrumptious smell filling the air.

"What on earth?" Chelsea stopped in the doorway of the kitchen, her voice trailing. She had never seen anything like it.

White chocolate mousse. Dark chocolate raspberry. Bananas Foster. Mocha chip. Butter pecan. Caramel cream. Chelsea's finest recipes lined the stainless steel island by the dozens. But they did not stop there. As Chelsea surveyed the room, the sugary confections seemed to have multiplied like the Gospel's loaves and fishes. There was enough to feed five thousand people (or at least a solid three hundred).

"Morning, boss."

Chelsea turned to see Manny standing behind her, covered in flour. "You did this?"

"I did not know which recipe you wanted to make, so I made them all." Manny shrugged, sending a puffy cloud of flour into the air.

"But there are over a hundred!" Chelsea exclaimed.

"You don't have to tell me," he said through a yawn. "I switched to half dozens after midnight."

"Wow . . ." she marveled. "You must really know how to stretch ingredients."

"A little lesson from my father. I come from a big family."

"Well, I don't know how you did it," Chelsea said, still shaking her head, "but they look *perfect*. Have you tried any of them?"

Manny nodded. "They're really good."

"Which ones?"

"Um, all of them." He gave Chelsea a sheepish grin. "But don't take it from me."

Chelsea bit into her personal favorite: a melt-in-your-mouth German chocolate recipe. It was heavenly. "But what will we do with them all?"

Chelsea spotted the reporter the moment he entered the café. Imposing frame, wire-rimmed glasses, and wiry hair just beginning to gray.

"Bill Davis. I used to work with your father. He doing okay?" he asked as they shook hands.

Only two topics were off-limits. Chelsea's father was the first.

Ding! Ding! She breathed a sigh of relief, thankful for the interruption. And for a customer to fill the empty café.

"Delivery for Chelsea Chambers!"

Chelsea raised her hand to identify herself. *Please don't be the IRS.*

"It's from Sawyer Chambers," the delivery woman added, handing Chelsea a small package.

Chelsea knew she should wait to open it. But how could she resist? "Excuse me a moment," she said to the reporter. Inside she found a folded note taped to a box of chocolates.

Sorry about everything. Especially losing our money. Working to fix it. Sawyer. P. S. I figured a box of chocolates didn't break the communication ban.

Chelsea's face burned hot with emotion. Lots of emotion.

"So how is Sawyer Chambers these days?"

Sawyer Chambers. The second off-limits topic.

"Looks like y'all are gettin' along real fine," Bill continued, nodding to Sawyer's romantic gesture. "Guess there's no substance to those Internet rumors, eh?"

Chelsea blinked and blanked. She was a deer caught in the headlights. Of a freight train. Bill might as well have been wearing a conductor's hat.

"Will he be around at all today?" The reporter wasn't giving up.

Splat! Manny dropped a box of cupcakes

on the floor right beside them, barely missing Bill's shoes. Chelsea jumped to her feet to retrieve the box, apologizing for Manny, yet never so grateful for his clumsiness. As she stood, Chelsea noticed the tall stack of boxes in his arms.

"These are all ready, Mrs. Chambers."

"Ready?" Chelsea asked.

"For your morning delivery."

Written on the side of each box was an address. Some Chelsea recognized, others she didn't.

Bill eyed the addresses. "The Salvation Army? La Bandera apartment complex? St. Vincent's assisted living . . . Hard to believe these places can even afford a special delivery."

Chelsea smiled at Manny. Finally, she got it.

"We're giving them away," she declared. "It was a part of my mom's weekly routine for decades. I'm just carrying on the tradition. Care to come along, Bill? I can drive. It'll give us a chance to talk." Chelsea took the boxes from Manny. "About the café," she emphasized.

Their trip through the surrounding community was an eye-opener. And not just for Bill, who scribbled Chelsea's every move into his pocket notebook. To Chelsea, this hardly seemed like the neighborhood of her childhood. At least not as she remembered it.

As young girls, Chelsea and Sara had volunteered with their mother at the local Salvation Army. But even on Thanksgiving Day there were never this many people waiting in line — nor so few volunteers there to serve them.

La Bandera apartments stood in shambles. Windows had been shuttered with plywood and cardboard, offering residents little shelter from the winter cold. The years of neglect were all the more striking when compared to the trendy high-income homes nearby.

At St. Vincent's, Chelsea and Bill were greeted by elderly residents who lit up at the sight of the cupcakes and who lingered for the company after the baked goods were gone.

Then she saw him. An old man seated by a window, jingling what appeared to be a set of keys. Charles Hancock, her father. But this was not the man in her memories. He was feeble and gray, his identity betrayed only by his deep brown eyes, the one physical trait Chelsea shared with her father.

Thirteen years had passed since Chelsea had last seen him. She could still recall his face, twisted with anger. His long-ago explosion still rocked her emotional world. Those distinctive eyes that had burned with rage. The voice that had roared with disappointment. *You're giving up all you've worked toward to be . . . what . . . a housewife!* It seemed like yesterday to Chelsea. But it looked like a lifetime on her father. A lifetime she was not ready to face.

Chelsea grabbed Bill's arm and headed for the door. "I've lost track of the time — I need to get back to the café."

When she jerked to a stop in the empty parking lot, Bill said his thanks and made a quick escape, leaving Chelsea with a moment alone. Her crowded mind needed the space. Her father was now occupying every nook and cranny, and she was eager to kick him out.

CHAPTER 9

CHURCH SHOPPING? WE'RE OPEN SUN-DAYS! boasted the marquee. Chelsea chuckled at her brother-in-law's wit. Pastor Tony Morales had a winsome personality and a lively sense of humor. It's no wonder he and Sara were such a good match.

With the newspaper interview behind her, Chelsea was following through on her promise to set up shop for Sunday service. Faith Community Church was only a five-minute drive from Higher Grounds. It sat south of the King William district in a neighborhood where houses were smaller, cars were older, and more than one front lawn served as a workshop for a shade-tree mechanic.

The congregation met in a former Baptist church. Worn concrete steps led up to the main entrance, and the red brick had long since faded to pink. A tall steeple adorned the roof.

Chelsea hadn't attended church often in the last decade. On Sundays, Sawyer was either recovering from a game or playing in one. During the off-season, he liked to golf or work out. He never wanted to go to church.

"It would just turn into a big autograph session," he would tell her. And he was right.

But Chelsea could get in and out without being recognized. She'd found a mega-church in Dallas where she could sign the kids in at the nursery and take a comfortable seat in the back of the sanctuary the size of an airplane hangar. The preacher looked like a munchkin on the large stage, so she watched on the big screen.

Today, as she led Hancock, Emily, and Manny through the weighty red doors of Faith Community, she was flooded with warm memories. The stained glass, the *Do This in Remembrance of Me* carving on the altar, the woody smell of old pews — it felt so familiar. Chelsea could almost hear her mother singing with vibrance and vibrato . . . *"It is well . . . It is well with my soul!"* No matter the trials her family faced, Chelsea had always found peace in the pews. This was one part of her family history she didn't mind revisiting.

"We're so glad you're here!" Sara welcomed them into the humble space. "We've got big plans for this church," she said. "Tony is such a visionary!"

Visionary indeed. Where Chelsea saw the dented walls and stained carpet of the old banquet hall, Tony envisioned a multimedia youth room. The cracked concrete basketball court was simply a "skatepark-to-be." The linoleum-floored lobby, an inviting coffee bar — that is, if Chelsea could add her magic touch.

"A city on a hill!" Tony said at the end of their tour. "That's how I see this place. If it brings the people to the church, I'm all for it!"

"I don't know that my café is going to make any converts, but I sure hope the reverse is true," Chelsea said to Manny as they set up in the lobby. "We could use the customers."

As the congregation filtered into the sanctuary, Chelsea had doubts that this crowd could get her business booming. First, there wasn't much of a crowd. Only one-third of the pews were occupied. Second, the average age appeared to be well over sixty. In spite of Tony's passion, this congregation was not thriving. It was barely surviving.

"Ask and it will be given to you; seek and

you will find . . ." Chelsea tuned into Tony's words.

There's something I can get behind. Chelsea knew what she'd ask God for. Answers. But the more she thought about it, the longer her list of questions grew. In fact, it outgrew the length of the service.

Chelsea was still pondering her questions when she lay in bed that night. But she never did bring herself to ask them.

CHAPTER 10

Watching and waiting. That's what Chelsea and Manny were doing the morning the newspaper review went to press. The *Tribune* was distributed weekly to cafés around town, and Chelsea wanted to be the first to read it.

If she couldn't make the business work, she needed a backup plan, and quick. She did have a few in mind. A tell-all memoir. A spiritual pilgrimage. A cooking blog. Buying a Tuscan chateau. All utterly sensible ways to undergo a midlife crisis, not to mention increase her odds of landing in the arms of a chiseled and contemplative (she wasn't entirely shallow) man. One who treasured her for all her flaws and eccentricities and extra weight.

Why not? It always worked for Julia Roberts.

The first payment to the IRS was due in three weeks, and the Higher Grounds Café had yet to meet its daily latte quota. Chelsea needed people lining up around the block.

Please, God. Is that too much to ask?

"Did you say something?" Manny asked.

"No, I just . . . We really need a glowing review."

Watching and waiting. Then a thud on the front porch.

"The paper boy!"

Chelsea and Manny raced for the door. The review of the Higher Grounds Café was the lead story in the Food and Dining section.

"This is it, Manny. The moment of truth." Chelsea took a deep breath and opened the paper right there on the front lawn.

"If the Higher Grounds Café manages to reinvent itself today, then it might still be around tomorrow," Chelsea recited from memory.

"I thought it was a nice review," Bo said, taking a sip of his cappuccino.

"What was that thing he said? About the fireplace?" asked Sara, who had dropped in to offer moral support after reading the review online.

Manny scanned the newspaper. " 'Chelsea Chambers and her staff glow with the warmth of a fireplace. Though, unlike her predecessors, Mrs. Chambers takes a bit of kindling . . .' "

"Okay, Manny, that's enough!" Sara interrupted. "See, Chelsea? You're a fireplace."

Chelsea was not glowing, and neither was the review. Sure, Bill Davis praised the café's generous spirit and commitment to the community, but he packaged these things as "the time-held traditions of a timeworn establishment." He called the coffee "acceptable" and the baked goods "divine," but said the café left much to be desired in the way of modern conveniences. In a neighborhood that valued slick design and high-speed Internet, he reckoned there was no longer room for nostalgia. The closing line was the real kicker: "Higher Grounds Café could become a hub in South San, but for now, it's a good old-fashioned café with a lot of heart."

Except there was a typo, so it read "God old-fashioned café."

"One good line, and it's not even quotable!" Chelsea shouted to the heavens in jest.

"God heard that," Sara said playfully. "And you know what? He even cares."

"And that, right there, is why you will live happily ever after," Chelsea said, her skepticism shining through. She could tell from the look on Sara's face that she had come off harsher than intended.

"Well, folks, I think I better relieve Tony." Sara attempted a smile. "Any chance I could get two Americanos?"

"One for Tony and one for you to hold?" Chelsea asked.

Sara grinned. "Maybe. Or one for each hand."

Sara left with three Americanos. Just in case.

Bo lingered in the café long after his cappuccino was gone. The hollow sound of his fingers drumming on the paper cup told Chelsea there was something on his mind.

"Can I get you anything, Bo?" she asked.

"Oh, no . . ."

Chelsea settled into the chair across from him. She had never seen him like this, but somehow she found comfort in the fact that a good man like Bo could be troubled by something. "Bo? Are you sure everything is okay?"

He seemed reluctant even to look at her. "No, Chelsea, I'm afraid it's not," he began, summoning a bit of boldness. "I've been coming into this café every day for the last seven years. During that time, I learned a lot about you from your mother. And I know exactly what she'd want me to say to you right now."

Chelsea sat back in her chair, her heart racing.

"I don't know everything you're going through. Just like you don't know everything I'm going through. But I can tell you, whatever it is, God can help. But you have to ask Him."

With that the reluctant evangelist got to his feet. "Now you'll have to excuse me, but I've got to leave. And I sure hope you let me come back after this," he added.

Chelsea was glued to her seat, searching for a response.

"I've tried, Bo," she said just before he reached the door. "I've tried to ask for help." She tilted her head and sighed. "Faith . . . well, faith is hard for me. I've got questions and, to be honest, I've made mistakes."

Bo spoke from some place deep within. "Try again," he said. "And keep trying. I can't promise that one prayer will change everything. But it might."

Chelsea thought she spotted moisture in his eyes. But he turned away before she knew for sure.

That night after the kids were asleep, Chelsea's mind returned to her ever-growing list of troubles. She wracked her brain for new solutions, but she had tried everything she could think to do.

Try again.

It had been a long time since Chelsea had prayed a prayer and meant it. She searched for the words to sum up her problems, but all she could think of was a phrase so simple she wasn't even sure it would count.

"God, I need help."

CHAPTER 11

"You certainly have sophisticated taste!" Chelsea said, adding a third shot of espresso to a steaming café breve.

"It's for my mom. It's her birthday," said the boy. He couldn't have been older than ten, eleven tops. But his eyes seemed wiser. His skinny frame appeared in desperate need of a warm jacket.

"How 'bout a hot chocolate for you? It's a little chilly outside."

"That's okay, I'm fine."

Chelsea scooped up the boy's pocket change. He was a quarter short of $3.55, but she wasn't going to count that against him. "I'm Chelsea. I don't think I've seen you before. Do you live around here?"

"I'm Marcus. I live a couple miles away."

Chelsea wondered if he had walked from La Bandera. "I tell you what, Marcus. Your hot chocolate's on the house today. And so are these blueberry muffins," she said, wrapping them up to go. For the last three days, Chelsea had thrown away stale leftover baked goods. She'd much rather see someone enjoy them while they were fresh.

"Really? Wow . . . Thank you, ma'am!" Marcus pulled his baseball cap over his mop of dark hair. "I'll be sure to come back here. To buy stuff," he added in earnest. "Hope to see you next week!"

"See you then," Chelsea said.

But the words felt false. She had taken a good hard look at her finances. The bottom line was this: Chelsea's days at the café were numbered. The month was coming to a close, and she was still $8,500 short of her payment to the IRS.

She glanced at the clock. Two hours before closing. One hundred forty-eight lattes short of her daily quota. "Manny!" she hollered. "I'm making the call."

Manny entered from the kitchen. "Closing for the day, boss?"

"I'm calling a realtor." Chelsea closed her eyes, collecting her emotions. "I'm closing the café. For good." She forced a smile. It was better than crying.

"Oh, Chelsea. No! You can't!" Manny proved far less capable at controlling his emotions. He fell into a chair, his shoulders slumped.

Chelsea comforted him with a few pats on the back. *Wait, is he crying? Shouldn't I be the one crying?*

"But what are you going to do now?" he asked.

A very good question. Chelsea could afford the first month's bill with the dwindling cash in her savings. If she could make a quick sale on the café, she would be free of her mother's debt. And after that? She couldn't afford to think that far ahead.

"Right now . . . we are going to clean this place up. You can help yourself to any of the baked goods."

Chelsea had been holding onto a real estate brochure touting the "Best of Alamo Heights" ever since Deb's birthday party. It was hard to believe a few short weeks ago her idea of a next step was purchasing a McMansion. She put in a call to the realtor listed on the back.

What kind of name was Dennis Darling?

Emily descended the stairs, a bag of baby carrots in her hand, just as Chelsea was wrapping up the call with Dennis. He seemed to live up to his name, at least on the phone.

"Hey, Mom?" Emily asked.

Chelsea put her finger to her lips and

pulled Emily onto her lap. "I'll see you tomorrow then," Chelsea said. "Oh, well, I look forward to meeting you too." She set down the phone.

"Why are you smiling, Mom?" Emily asked.

"I'm not," Chelsea said, reining in the grin that had crept onto her face.

"Oh. What's wrong with Manny?"

Chelsea followed Emily's gaze. A sniffling Manny disappeared into the kitchen with a warm, gooey chocolate lava cake. "Oh, I think Manny's just really . . . hungry."

"We need to get him some healthy snacks," Emily said.

Ding! Ding! Two striking figures entered the café, a brawny, dark-skinned man accompanied by a towering woman with blond hair and blazing blue eyes.

"Wow," Emily said. "Are you from the Olympics?"

The woman smiled. "We're here to upgrade your Internet service."

Chelsea couldn't place her accent. Dutch? Norwegian, maybe? "I'm afraid I didn't ask for any upgrade." Chelsea stood, placing Emily back on the seat. "Manny?"

Manny moped into the café, still chomping on cake. But upon seeing the visitors, his mouth emptied. Like a chocolate volcano. Chelsea knew she wouldn't be making lava cake again for a very long while.

"Do you know anything about an Internet upgrade?" she asked him.

Manny gave a tentative nod. "Is it the plan that's free of charge for the first three months?"

"That's the one." The man's biceps bulged as he opened a metal case. "Best connection we offer," he said, placing a gleaming sphere on the table in front of Chelsea.

"It's beautiful!" Manny marveled at the curious device. "But smaller than I imagined." His fingers hovered inches above the object. "May I touch it?"

Had Manny lost his mind?

"Let's not touch anything yet. It looks expensive," Chelsea said. "What are the terms? Do I have to sign something?"

"No, it's a just a trial period. If you wish to discontinue our service in three months, we'll remove the router. No questions, no charges."

Chelsea wasn't convinced. "I'm not really big on the Internet. Besides, I probably won't even be here in three months."

"Where will we be, Mom?" Hancock asked. Chelsea hadn't even seen him come downstairs.

"With Daddy?" Emily perked up.

"That's enough, everybody!" After a long day of hard decisions, Chelsea's patience had worn thin. She turned to the serviceman. "*No* additional charges?"

"Absolutely none," he said.

Chelsea picked up the router. "How fast can you install it?"

"Before you can say amen," he said with a smile.

Chelsea watched the duo walk out the door. Pushy salespeople rubbed her the wrong way. Especially ones that looked like supermodels. And now everything was bothering her. Even Manny.

He was sweeping the floor around her feet, whistling a jolly tune. What did he have to be so cheerful about? But then again, what did it matter now? There was a much harder conversation ahead.

"C'mon, kiddos," Chelsea said. "Let's go get supper."

She was halfway up the stairs when the front door sounded the arrival of a customer. *My final customer,* she thought. She sent the kids to set the table and ceremoniously prepared "the last latte of the Higher Grounds Café" for a pensive patron named Miles, who had introduced himself and settled in with his laptop at a corner table.

"Your Internet's broken," he announced in a deep, booming voice as Chelsea delivered his latte. His eyes never left his screen.

"That's impossible!" Manny cried, dropping his broom and running to the man's side. At the sight of the screen, Manny squealed like a schoolgirl.

"What?" Chelsea asked. "What is it, Manny?"

"It's perfect!"

Miles grimaced. "No, it's broken, I assure you. I can only get to one website."

"Well, let's just hope it's a good one," Chelsea joked.

"Trust me," Manny said with a grin. "You won't be disappointed."

CHAPTER 12

Church bells rang in the distance. It was midnight, but Manny couldn't sleep. Not tonight. He sat upright on his simple cot and looked out the window. Stars pierced the veil of the nighttime sky. Diamonds on a cloth of black velvet. Infinite. Innumerable, they seemed. And yet Manny knew different.

Each star, numbered. Each star, named!

Like every grain of sand. Every hair on his head. Every trouble that filled his day. Created. Numbered. Known.

"Samuel?" An explosion of light filled the room. "Or should I say, Manny?"

Manny squinted, his eyes adjusting to the starburst. *Gabriel!* He tried to stand, only his feet wouldn't let him. His wobbly knees melted to the floor. But the hair on the back of his neck was standing tall. *Typical human reaction.*

"Sorry. Still getting used to all this,"

Manny said, motioning to his body.

Gabriel offered Manny a hand, pulling him to his feet. "It takes a while."

Gabriel's towering presence filled the room. His form was solid and sculpted, yet translucent, as if carved from light itself. Unblemished sunlight. His eyes blazed like a cosmic storm, creating an aurora dazzling as the northern lights. For the first time Manny could appreciate just how majestic, terrifying even, the sight of a spiritual being appears to the human eye.

"So *you've* been grounded before?" Manny asked. The look on Gabriel's face told him. "Of course, of course. You're not allowed to say."

"I can say this: some of my finest moments were in human form."

Manny leaned forward. "Any missions I'd know about?"

"Let's just say I can describe the many colors of Joseph's coat, and the house of Martin Luther, and tell you what Abe Lincoln ate for breakfast."

"I had a hunch those were your missions!"

"But I am not here to talk about me. I am here to see how you are doing. Your plan is off to a great start."

"It is? From where I'm sitting, it looks like we might be too late. Chelsea's closing

81

the café."

"We were held up," Gabriel explained. "Encountered far more resistance than we anticipated. Michael was even sent to help us."

Manny's jaw hit the floor. "Michael, as in Archangel Michael? I knew it! I knew it was him in the café!"

"That wasn't Michael."

"Really? Huh." Manny went back to his musing. "Still . . . me and Michael. Working on the same mission. I wish I could've seen what you saw."

"Who says you can't?" Gabriel stepped forward and placed his hand on Manny's shoulder.

At the moment of Gabriel's touch, Manny's eyes were opened to a new dimension. Recent events unfolded as if on-screen, this time from heaven's view. Manny saw himself serving lattes and sweeping floors, and all the while a conflict was brewing around him. Faceless figures, shrouded in darkness, dashed through streets and jumped from rooftop to rooftop. They left shadows in their wake that spread over the houses like soot. But just as they laid claim to the territory, angels appeared. Strong, glowing, golden figures descended onto the streets. At their coming, the demons turned and stopped.

"Do you see why we're here, Manny?" Gabriel asked.

Manny looked into his superior's face and shook his head.

Gabriel touched the angel's arm again. "Look closer."

Manny saw the faces and heard the voices of some people he had come to know and love.

Bo, seated in his pickup in front of the café, his head bowed as he leaned over the steering wheel. "Father, send strength to this place."

Sara, standing on the lawn looking toward Chelsea's window, her cheeks moistened with tears. "Bless my sister, O Lord."

Tony, striding through the neighborhood. In a quiet, but firm voice he prayed, "Come, Lord!"

And Chelsea. Manny's heart jumped when, in his vision, he saw Chelsea praying. She was sitting on the porch late at night. Her face seemed empty of hope.

"God, I need help."

"Their prayers were heard?" Manny said to Gabriel.

"Each and every one."

As Manny watched the events unfold, he saw himself getting caught up in the action.

He bobbed and turned, swinging an invisible sword, as if he were in the middle of it all. Then a bolt of light sent a shock through the atmosphere.

"Michael!" Manny exclaimed as he watched heaven's most powerful angel take on the forces of darkness. The angels fell into formation around him, confusing the enemy. And then . . .

"Now!" At the sound of Michael's voice, the angels pierced the darkness with a tunnel of light, creating a gateway between the heavens and the café. Angels encircled the column and stood guard.

Heaven is fighting for them. Manny was captivated by the thought. But his vision began to blur.

"Manny . . . Manny?"

Manny looked up at Gabriel. For the second time that day, the smaller angel had tears in his eyes. "This mission is big, isn't it?"

"Immense. But that's just it, Manny. They all are."

When Gabriel left, Manny's mind was racing. Not with doubts, but questions, for the two are not the same. Even the deepest, darkest questions can lead to a deeper faith. But still, there was so much he couldn't see. So much he didn't know. But one thing he did. Even in the darkest of nights, he could always look up.

That night, Manny fell asleep counting the stars.

Chapter 13

Chelsea looked down at a rainbow of colored Sharpie markers, searching for a cheerful spin on the bad news. But no matter how many adjectives her inner thesaurus conjured, Hancock and Emily were unconvinced that their future was "bright," "exciting," "promising," or "adventurous."

"Are we gonna be okay?" Her son's stare cut to the bone.

"Of course we're gonna be okay," Chelsea said, but she wasn't convinced. And from the fearful look in her daughter's eyes, neither was Emily. Chelsea took her daughter's hand. "Because we have each other. And I'm going to figure this out."

But after hours of wracking her brain, she was still stumped. And the poster board on the dinner table was still blank. Her sister's phone call was a welcome distraction.

"Just calling to see how you're doing," Sara said.

"I'm okay. I think. I hope. It's just that this place is special, you know? I hate that it's ending with me. I feel like I'm letting Mom down. Grandma too."

"Well, you can't take all the blame. Mom did leave you with a pretty hefty tab. And as for Grandma . . . I had her jewelry appraised. I figured I could sell it. Help you pay off the debt."

"I would never accept!"

"Well, you won't have to. It's costume jewelry. All of it!"

Chelsea sighed. "When we were growing up I knew times were tough, but I had this fantasy it was all part of some Cinderella story. It was just a matter of time before Prince Charming would come and whisk me away. Clearly, that didn't happen, but I at least thought my days of pinching pennies were over."

"Hey, don't give up on your fairy-tale ending. I have a backup plan."

"Oh yeah?"

"I'm winning the lottery on Tuesday."

Chelsea laughed. "Go to bed. I'll talk to you later."

Chelsea stared again at the expanse of blank poster board. And then it hit her. She grabbed the black marker. Her bold strokes squeaked across the shiny white surface.

No more sugar coating. No more rainbow-hued nostalgia. It was time to face the facts and move on with life.

Chelsea appraised her handiwork. There it was. The simple truth in black-and-white. THE HIGHER GROUNDS CAFÉ HAS GONE OUT OF BUSINESS.

Early Saturday morning, a weary Chelsea descended the stairs, coffee in one hand, poster and tape in the other. She was thankful for her first day of rest in nearly four months. She hadn't bothered to change out of her robe and slippers. Her hair was unbrushed and her face untouched. There'd be no customers to impress. No coffee to serve. No spills to clean up. Or so she thought.

Midway down the stairs she stopped. Her coffee mug slipped from her fingers and cracked on the hardwood floor.

People were everywhere. Through the front windows she saw multitudes gathering on the porch, spilling out into the lawn in a sea of heads bent over smartphones, laptops, and tablets. The neighborhood was abuzz with activity. And at the center of it all was the Higher Grounds Café.

CHAPTER 14

"I don't know what's happening," Chelsea said to Sara over speakerphone. "But it's like Walmart on Black Friday!" She and the kids peered at the rapidly growing crowd through the blinds of Hancock and Emily's bedroom window.

"They're everywhere, Aunt Sara!" Hancock added.

"I've worked in retail," Sara said. "Seize the moment. Open up the shop!"

Chelsea tallied the crowd. A hundred lattes, easy. "It would be nice to go out with a bang," Chelsea said. "Let me give Manny a ring."

His response was immediate: "I'll be there in a heartbeat!"

An eavesdropper would have thought Chelsea had offered him a dream vacation or a winning lottery ticket rather than an extra day's work. His enthusiasm was odd. Then again, it was Manny. Chelsea sighed and whispered to herself, "Help is on the way."

She brushed her teeth, threw on her go-to outfit of sweatshirt and jeans, and ventured downstairs.

She opened the door and stepped through the crowd. "Excuse me. Excuse me." As she reached the front of the the porch she shouted, "Hello, everyone!" No response. So, louder. "Helloooo!"

Heads snapped up from their technology. What an assorted lot of age, skin color, and status. Housewives, students, and business-men. All eyes were on her, and for a split second Chelsea questioned whether she had indeed remembered to change out of her robe into pants. She felt for pockets. *Whew.*

"Welcome to the Higher Grounds Café! We will be —"

"Hey, lady. Are you the one answering the questions?" called one of the squatters, as he tossed a cigarette butt on her trampled lawn.

"What ques—" Chelsea started.

"Is it really God?" shouted a teenager.

"Of course it's God!" an old woman called from the front porch. "Right?" she asked, directing her question at Chelsea.

"I . . . what are you talking about? I don't really know."

"I'll give you one hundred bucks if I can ask another question!" The offer came from a middle-aged man whose laptop was sitting on the hood of a fancy sports car.

His comment sparked a frenzy.

"We can *buy* more questions?"

"That's not fair!"

The front lawn turned to chaos. Everyone talked at once, and they all seemed to forget who they were talking to in the first place. No one noticed Chelsea disappear into the café.

"Are all those people coming inside?" Hancock asked. Emily bounded down the stairs behind him.

"Well, if they're not here to buy coffee, then I don't want them on our lawn!" Chelsea said. "Something's going on with that router."

Hancock and Emily followed Chelsea into the storage closet.

"Whoa!" Hancock saw it first.

The wireless router still sat between stacks of napkins and bags of coffee beans, but its appearance had changed. The glowing sphere was buzzing with energy and activity. Like a web of firing synapses, bursts of blue light danced within the orb. It had the look of lightning in a thundercloud and the whirling sound of a small fan.

The trio stood motionless. "What's it doing, Mom?" Emily asked.

"I have no idea, sweetie."

The device cast a glow on their faces as they leaned in for a closer look. Chelsea reached for the power cable.

"Are you sure you should do that?" Hancock asked.

"We're about to find out." She yanked the plug, and the orb went dark and fell silent.

Chelsea marched back onto the porch, holding the lifeless router in her hands. Confusion was rippling through the crowd. "Hey! What happened to the God Blog?"

The God Blog?

Chelsea had no idea what they were talking about, but she had their attention. "Look, people. I want paying customers, not *praying* customers. Start lining up, and I'll plug this thing back in. Got it?"

Like sheep answering to a shepherd's voice, the people flocked to the door of the café and formed a line down the sidewalk. But no one was more eager to get the Internet back up and running than Manny, who had just arrived at the café out of breath and grinning like a golden retriever. He was dressed for action in a John Deere hat, high-top sneakers, and a nylon tracksuit circa 1993.

Chelsea couldn't help but laugh. "Where in the world do you find your clothes, Manny? Do you buy them at garage sales?"

"No, but I appreciate the tip," he said.

Just then an elderly Hispanic woman approached Chelsea, speaking Spanish at a fast clip. Her charcoal braid was striking against the vibrantly colored, embroidered floral scarf she pulled tight around her shoulders. Chelsea attempted to follow the woman's words, but gave up after a few sentences.

Manny came to her aid, placing a calming hand on the woman's arm. The certainty in his voice seemed to soothe her. She took her place in line with the other customers, though her arched brow and suspicious gaze pinned her as a skeptic among believers.

Chelsea gave Manny a questioning look.

"She asked why all the people are here," he said.

"And what did you tell her?"

"Vinieron a buscar a Dios," he said. "They came to look for God." Manny stepped off the porch and into the lingering crowd on the lawn. "All right, everyone! You heard the woman! Line up, line up!" He herded the customers toward the front door.

"Excuse me?"

Chelsea turned to see a good-looking man

with salt-and-pepper hair. "Sir, I'm going to have to ask you to wait in line with everyone else."

"I didn't realize other realtors were up for the job," he said with a smirk.

"Dennis Darling!" Chelsea said, seizing his hand with a hearty shake. "I can't believe I forgot our appointment. Today is a little . . . well, as you can see, it's crazy!"

"I'd be happy to come back later. Say, dinnertime? We can have a bite, discuss your needs, and then take a look around the house."

"Wow, that sounds very . . . personal," Chelsea said with a chuckle.

"It's the Dennis Darling way. Do you like pizza?"

"I do," she said. "And so do my kids," she added for good measure.

"Great. I'll be back around seven."

Dennis was confident and collected and impossibly attractive. Chelsea tried to imagine him losing his cool, but she could not. Must be the Dennis Darling way. She watched heads turn as he weaved through the café. Dennis did not walk; he cruised. But he was not the only one cruising.

Behind the counter, Manny was single-handedly servicing a line of customers that went out the door. He was steaming milk, grinding coffee, ringing up orders; he was a one-man band. His tracksuit swished in perfect time. *Puff! Whirr! Swish! Cha-ching!* Where Manny's sudden burst of coordination came from, Chelsea had no idea, but she couldn't help but hum her own tune.

"Boss, are you singing? It's about time!" Manny exclaimed.

"Well, it's the grand finale. I'm pulling out all the stops," she said, tying an apron around her waist. "Now let's sell some coffee!"

As Chelsea and Manny served one customer after another, they pieced together the mystery behind the masses. The God Blog, as it had been coined, was first discovered by the host of San Antonio's number one radio show, "Miles in the Morning."

"He was in here last night. I knew I recognized that voice!" Chelsea exclaimed to one of his faithful listeners.

After his visit, Miles told all of San Antonio they could talk to God by logging onto the Internet at the Higher Grounds Café. And so the people came, each one armed with a question — the one big question they would be allowed to ask God and actually get God's answer. Chelsea was amazed by the number of people who bought this story, no questions asked. (Except, of course, for the question they asked God.)

The God Blog had its fair share of skeptics, of course, even the first day. Chelsea spotted a huddle of people standing on the front lawn with crossed arms and concerned expressions. But for every skeptic she also encountered a believer, and sometimes the former became the latter.

"Dios escuchó mis oraciones." The same Spanish-speaking woman reached over the counter and pulled Chelsea into an embrace. *"Dios escuchó mis oraciones!"* she exclaimed through tears.

"She says that God heard her prayers," Manny translated.

"Oh, well I'm very happy for her," Chelsea said, extracting herself from the woman's vise-like grip. "You can tell her that."

But the weepy woman rattled on, never giving Manny the chance.

"She says she had given up on God. But today God showed her that He cares. He even remembers her silent prayers."

When the woman had finished her story, she unwrapped the floral scarf from around her shoulders and handed it to Chelsea.

"It's a gift," Manny said. "For you."

Chelsea could only smile as she received the sincere gift. She couldn't explain what was happening, but she certainly could not deny it.

CHAPTER 15

"So I told Mr. Darling that I'm just not interested in selling the place!" Chelsea said. "Not yet, anyway. I mean, we made half of this month's tax payment in one day. One day! We even ran out of coffee. I actually had to unplug the router to get people to go home!"

Tony and Sara sat opposite Chelsea and the kids, two open pizza boxes courtesy of Dennis Darling between them. "By the way, you guys should talk to Dennis about your house. He seems like the go-to guy in real estate these days."

"Actually," Sara said, a smile breaking onto her face, "we accepted an offer this afternoon!"

"Congratulations! We have so many reasons to celebrate today!" Chelsea exclaimed. "Did I tell you there was a thousand dollars in the tip jar? Can you believe it?"

Tony cleared his throat. "It certainly is

hard to believe," he ruminated, planting a firm gaze on his sister-in-law. "I'm all for marketing the place, Chelsea. But this idea of yours . . ."

Chelsea sat up straight. "I didn't make this up, Tony. Come on, let me show you." She ushered her family inside the supply pantry. "I just plug it in, and it starts glowing." Chelsea wrangled the cables. "Like this."

The room filled with blue light. Tony ventured a closer look at the glowing router. "No brand name. No numbers. Nothing. Where did you say it came from?"

"No idea. I assumed the company info would be on the router, but it's not."

"So when people come to the café, there's only one site that works?" Tony asked.

"Yep."

"And when people ask a question, someone answers?" Sara asked.

"Why don't you see for yourself?"

Sara read aloud from the blog's headline: "Go ahead, ask me. I will answer."

"That's it? And people fall for this?" Tony said, peering over Sara's shoulder.

"Apparently." Sara swiped through the entries on her tablet screen.

Question: You aren't for real, right? If you

were for real, you would have heard my prayers weeks ago. Since the mill closed, I still have no job, no interviews. I have sent hundreds of résumés. My wife is worried. I have kids and a mortgage, and I have many, many doubts.

Answer: Suppose your child said something similar to you. "You aren't my real dad. I've been asking for a new bike for a month. A real dad would give me one." Is the real dad the one who does what the child wants? No, he's the one who does what is right for the child.

That is what I do. I know you are tired. Just be patient. I hear your prayers. And I know the foreman at the other plant.

Question: I have trouble sleeping at night. I can't get my mind off of all the challenges I will face the next day. Why can't I sleep?

Answer: Your nights are long because you carry too much fear. I've been watching you. Why don't you give those fears to me? Stop trying to fix everyone (including your husband) and figure everything out. And I haven't heard you laugh in quite a while. Lighten up. I love it when you are happy. Remember, come to me when you are weary and tired. I can help you.

Sara looked up from her tablet. "Can't say I disagree," she said.

"But still, replying to someone's questions, saying you're God? That seems like a crass way to market a website," Tony added.

Sara continued reading the questions:

Why can't I make sense out of my life? My husband neglects me. How can I get his attention?

"Here's one that's really profound," she said.

"God, are you really there?"
  "Yes, I am."

Chelsea laughed. "At least whoever's answering these has a sense of humor."

"Dear God, money's been real tight for Carla and me with all the medical bills. I got $800 left in savings. Any chance you could give me a hint at what slot machine to play tonight? I promise to give you half! Love, Bronson."

"Dear Bronson, Instead of gambling away the last of your savings, why not use it to pay your mortgage and whittle down the debt? Trust me. Seek wisdom. Give me a chance to provide. And please tell

Carla I said hello. It makes me happy to see her recovering from surgery. Love, God."

"Wow. That's pretty strong," Sara commented.

"And specific," Chelsea said.

"Does God know everything?" Emily asked.

"Of course he does," Tony answered. "But he wouldn't be answering people's questions on some silly blog." Tony turned to Chelsea. "It's got to be an algorithm. Someone could be stealing your customers' information, using Internet cookies or something."

"But why would anyone do that here?" Chelsea added.

"Look, Tony! It's from Miles," Sara said.

"On the off chance this isn't some scam, here goes . . . Dear God, I feel so distant from my son. He's obsessed with video games. I got so mad at him the other day, I threw all his games into the pool. He actually said he hates me, and he's threatening to run away. Help. Miles."

"Dear Miles, Why worry about the video game in your son's eye, but not the laptop in yours? Hang out with Matthew. He just

wants your attention. You might be surprised at how much he longs to spend
one-on-one time with you. And now that
I've mentioned it, the same applies to me!
Hope to speak with you soon. Love, God."

"So how many questions can you ask?"
Hancock seemed eager to try the God Blog
for himself.

"Just one. According to the customers."

"Okay, so what if I asked a question on
my phone, and then borrowed my friend's
phone to ask another?"

"Lots of people tried that," Chelsea said,
"but it didn't work. It's like . . . somehow
the blog knew."

Tony clicked off the tablet and tucked it
away in a tight-fitting case. "Okay, shoot
straight with us. Who's writing these?"

"It's just me and Manny here. You really
think it's one of us?"

"Obviously it's someone in the café," Tony
said. "That's the logical explanation!"

"Well, you could just . . . try it," Chelsea
said.

"Good idea," Sara said, grabbing the
tablet from Tony. "C'mon, this'll be fun.
Who has a question?"

Emily and Hancock had lots of ideas.

"Ask about the tooth fairy!"

"No, dinosaurs. Or aliens. No, wait! Do you care if we go to school?" Hancock asked.

"That's not a question," Chelsea said.

"I have one," Tony said. "If this is really God, then why speak through a blog?"

"Good one!" Chelsea said.

"All right, Tony's question wins." Sara clicked away on the tablet screen, posting the question to the mysterious blog. The entire gang gathered around, anticipating the reply.

"There it is!" Hancock yelled.

Sara pulled the tablet close and read aloud.

"Dear Tony, Have you ever wondered why I answered Gideon with a fleece and Balaam with a donkey? Why did I speak to Job with a strong wind and Elijah with a still voice? I directed Moses with a cloud and the Magi with a star. Why? Answer those questions and you'll find the answer to yours."

"Wow," Sara said as she put down the tablet. "How's that for an answer?"

"Anyone coulda written that!" Tony said.

"Maybe. But it was your question that I typed. And it answered with 'Dear Tony'!

How could it possibly know?"

"Because it's my tablet. Like I said, it's an algorithm or something."

But Hancock had the simplest explanation of all. "Maybe it's God."

CHAPTER 16

Chelsea was awakened by the smell of freshly brewed coffee. She opened her eyes to find Emily inches from her face with a big smile and a steaming mug towering with whipped cream.

"I made you a latte," Emily said, pushing the mug toward her mom. "You can do it really quick in the microwave."

"Wow . . . thank you." Chelsea shook the sleep from her eyes. Two weeks of nonstop traffic in the café had taken it out of her. Thanks to the God Blog, Higher Grounds was now running solid twelve-hour shifts, seven days a week. For the first time in months, Chelsea had room to breathe. At least in the area of finances. She made her first two payments to the IRS ahead of schedule and invested the month's extra income into a second commercial-grade oven, allowing her and Manny to produce more of their bestselling baked goods. Still, an unsettling question lingered in the back of Chelsea's mind. How long could this last?

The café's newfound success had nothing to do with Chelsea and everything to do with the God Blog. She could not control, predict, or even explain it. But neither could she deny it. Faith didn't come easy for her, yet she found herself living by faith each and every day — which must have added to her exhaustion because, for the second time that week, she had dozed off after her final sweep of the kitchen.

"How long have I been sleeping?" she asked, taking a sip of solid whipped cream.

"Um . . . I finished three math problems."

So at least thirty minutes.

"Good job, sweetheart!" Chelsea exclaimed. "Why don't we get some dinner and finish the rest together? I have a little math homework to do too." She led Emily back to the kitchen.

"*Bueno,*" Emily said. "Hancock *para va la* . . . Chinese food."

"He did what?"

"He went to get Chinese food for dinner. But don't worry, he has your wallet."

"He left? Why didn't he wake me up?"

"He said you don't like Chinese food."

"Never leave without asking me," Chelsea said firmly. "Got it?"

Emily nodded. "Is Hancock in trouble?"

"Why would I be in trouble?" Hancock appeared in the door of the kitchen with two weighty grocery bags.

"You can't leave without permission," Chelsea scolded. "You know that."

Hancock gave a weary shrug. "You looked tired."

Chelsea opened her mouth to unload her frustration, but she was stopped by the growing suspicion that Hancock's young shoulders were carrying all the weight they could bear. She motioned to the grocery bags. "I thought you were getting Chinese food."

"I was. But I thought I should get things we actually needed instead. We were out of everything."

Chelsea was hit with a pang of guilt. Getting to the grocery store had been on her to-do list for over a week.

"I ran into Bo, and he offered to drive me home, so I just loaded up on a bunch of stuff." Hancock gestured into the café, where an uncomfortable Bo lingered with two more grocery bags in his arms.

"Sorry if that caused any trouble," Bo said.

"No, no," Chelsea said, waving off his apology. "Everyone's trying to help. But we need to work on our communication. Make sure we're all speaking the same language. Understand?" Chelsea planted her gaze on Hancock. Before he could answer, Emily chimed in.

"Intiendo!"

The others chuckled.

"What? Did I say it wrong?"

"You said just the right thing," Chelsea replied, drawing both kids in for a hug. "So, what's for dinner?"

"That's where I come in," Bo said. "I make a mean marinara. And Hancock here says he has mastered the art of boiling spaghetti. So if you ladies don't mind leavin' the cooking to the men tonight, we'll have dinner ready in no time."

Now Bo was really speaking Chelsea's language.

"You're pretty quiet up there, Hancock," Chelsea said, slipping out of the bottom bunk bed. Emily had just finished a riveting retelling of her favorite story, "*La Princesa y la* . . . Pea." She was giving a big presentation in reading class the next day and wanted to practice. Chelsea was pleased to see her daughter's growing ease with Spanish.

Hancock didn't answer, and Chelsea stood up to find him lying on the top bunk, his eyes set on the ceiling. "Everything okay?" she asked.

Hancock gave a deep sigh and turned to face his mom. Chelsea was not yet fluent in twelve-year-old boy, but she was fairly certain this meant he was ready to talk.

"Did something happen at school? Trouble with friends?"

"I don't have any friends. So no. But that's just . . . whatever. I came late, and everybody already had friends."

Chelsea felt for him. All the changes had been hard enough on her; she could not imagine going through them as a middle schooler. "So what's on your mind?"

Hancock propped himself up on his elbow. "It's just . . . all about the café all the time. I want things to go back to normal."

"I know it's been busy, but this is a learning phase. We're all learning a new normal."

"Why can't we just go back to the old normal?"

Her son knew perfectly well it was a loaded question. And even though he knew the answer, he couldn't help asking. Tonight the truth was welling up in his watery blue eyes.

"We have to keep moving forward. Besides, you don't want a mom who can't run a business or take care of her family,"

Chelsea said, giving his hand a reassuring squeeze. "But I promise I'll carve out some time just for us. Even if I have to hire some extra help."

"You really promise?" he asked in a small, shaky voice.

"I *really* promise," Chelsea said. And she really meant it.

Hancock must have heard it in her voice, because a heavy burden seemed to lift from his chest as the words left her mouth. Then and there, Chelsea knew that whatever she had to do to keep her promise would be well worth it.

CHAPTER 17

"It was the planet Saturn that brought me here. This morning's horoscope compelled me to seek 'art, vitality, and value' in my occupational pursuits. When I looked up from the paper, I saw it. The sign was right there in front of me."

Chelsea's curiosity was piqued. "What kind of sign?"

"The sign for the Higher Grounds Café," Katrina said. "It was uncanny. Although it helped that Saturn's orbit was working in my favor. I'm a Scorpio."

"Right."

Katrina was Chelsea's third interview for the newly opened position at the café. She wore beads, a tie-dye shirt, and a long flowing skirt. Her angular face was framed by a shock of red hair, and her eyes and lips were painted with shimmering silver.

"And you expect to find art, vitality, and value working at a café?"

"Why wouldn't I?" Katrina asked. "Coffee is the most traded commodity in the world — second only to oil."

"Wow, I had no idea!"

"A person can live a day without silver or gold, but coffee? No thanks."

"I couldn't agree with you more," Chelsea said.

She had a good feeling about Katrina. She called Manny to the table and made the introduction. "Looks like you'll have a new barista buddy! This is Katrina. After all the other candidates, I'm convinced she's heaven sent. Any questions for her before you guys start?"

Manny assessed the young woman. Judging by her unique appearance, there was a fifty-fifty chance she was indeed sent from above. But there was only one way to find out. Manny crossed his arms and fired off a round of loaded questions.

"Where are you from?"

"Just moved here from Phoenix."

"And who do you report to?"

"My Uncle Frank, I guess. I'm living with him."

"What do you know about the God Blog?"

"The what? I'm not good with computers."

"Are you good with people?"

"Not as good as you," Katrina said drily.

Manny's smile cracked through his tough-guy facade. Moments later, Katrina was working alongside him behind the counter.

CHAPTER 18

Compared to talkative Manny, Katrina was a woman of few words, but she wasn't shy or sheepish. She just preferred her work, or her "art" as she called it, to do the talking. And what a rich conversationalist she could be! As a thank-you for hiring her, Katrina crafted Chelsea her favorite drink, a simple latte. Only this latte was anything but simple.

Chelsea watched as Katrina pulled two shots of espresso into the blank canvas of a white mug. She steamed the milk to perfection. But she didn't just dump it over the espresso willy-nilly. Oh no. Katrina thumped the stainless steel pitcher on the counter, dispersing the unsightly big bubbles of milk. She tipped the white liquid into the mug, her wrist twisting back and forth. Seconds later, Katrina unveiled her masterpiece: a latte topped with the coffee foam image of the planet Saturn.

"This is beautiful! Thank you, Katrina."

Chelsea was grateful. With Katrina, Chelsea had enough added margin in her day to tend to the baked goods in her new oven and even share a lunch with her kids. And much to Chelsea's delight, her patrons were just as appreciative of her new hire.

The first afternoon rush was a lively family who had recently been relocated to San Antonio. Their accents placed them as New Yorkers, so Katrina served them with a taste of home: cappuccinos emblazoned with the Statue of Liberty. The father left a fifty-dollar tip.

In the lull that followed, Katrina watched, transfixed, as the family of New Yorkers logged onto the God Blog, and then gathered together to offer tear-filled prayers up to heaven.

Chelsea asked her, "Have you tried the God Blog yet?"

"No. Only asking one question . . . that's a lot of pressure. Is it really real?"

"Of course it's real!" Manny interjected. "Is it *so* hard to believe that God is answering people's questions through a blog in your café?"

"Well, now that you put it that way . . ." Chelsea began, but then she and Katrina dissolved into laughter.

"Think about it," Manny said. "The Creator of the Universe is willing to answer your deepest question . . . and you're not even willing to ask? What if God really *is* on the other end of that Internet connection?"

Chelsea pondered Manny's audacious logic. But only for a moment. The lights in the café had begun to flicker and then . . . *ZAP!* All dark.

With the light from her cell phone, Chelsea inspected the circuit breaker in the pantry. She flipped some switches, but to no avail. She needed an expert.

"Sorry, folks!" she announced. "Looks like we're closing early today!"

Katrina and Manny distributed consolation cupcakes to exiting customers, while Chelsea took her son's suggestion to call their neighbor for some expert help.

Bo came at once, flashlight in hand. "I 'spect that's your problem right there," he said, illuminating Chelsea's new industrial oven. "You're fortunate a fire didn't break out. Gotta be careful of aluminum wiring in old houses like this."

"So what do you think it'll cost me to fix it?" Chelsea braced herself for the worst.

"Shouldn't be more than a hundred bucks. In a few hours I'll have the wiring to the oven redone. I still suggest you get all the aluminum replaced, but this'll hold you over till then."

"You mean you'll do this for us?"

"On one condition."

"Yeah?"

Bo pointed his flashlight at Hancock and Emily. "You take these young'uns out for the night. I think y'all could use a break."

Chelsea couldn't have been more pleased. It had only taken forty-eight hours for her to fulfill the promise she'd made to Hancock to carve out some time for family fun.

Forty-eight hours! I'd like to see Sawyer beat that.

That Hancock's favorite movie was playing at a local "oldies" theater was simply icing on the cake. "Four tickets to *Star Wars*, please."

Upon Manny's shocking admission that he had never seen *Star Wars*, Hancock had insisted that he come as their family's plus one. Chelsea wasn't sure what her children enjoyed more, watching the movie or watching Manny watch the movie. Emily and Hancock howled with laughter when Manny jumped with panic at the sight of Darth Vader, spilling his bucket of popcorn all over their laps. He took the passing of Obi Wan Kenobi especially hard, but when Luke launched the proton torpedoes into the Death Star, they couldn't keep him in his seat.

When they returned home, Chelsea was relieved to see the electricity working just as Bo had promised. He'd left a note, and just below his name he had scribbled a familiar passage of Scripture: *The Lord is near to all who call upon Him. Psalm 145:18*

Chelsea closed her eyes and reveled in the moment. For the first time in a very long time, she didn't feel helpless or alone. She had the help she needed at the café. Bo was proving to be quite the guardian angel. Even Hancock and Emily were settling into their family's new normal.

She ventured upstairs to tuck the kids into bed. But just before opening their door, something stopped her. The sweet sound of their laughter.

"It was hilarious!" Hancock said. "You have to meet him, Dad! He was yelling and cheering the whole time!"

"Popcorn spilled all over us!" Emily added.

Even over speakerphone, Sawyer's laughter echoed into the hall.

"I wish you coulda been there, Dad."

Sawyer. Chelsea still didn't know how he fit into their new normal.

"Hey, maybe next family fun night, you can come!" Hancock said.

"That sounds fun to me! But you should probably leave that for Mom to decide."

CHAPTER 19

Manny had to look closely, but he could see it. An image emerging within his cup. He held his breath as he worked, angling his mug side to side as the ivory liquid marbled the velvety espresso. He had picked up some impressive moves from Katrina over the last week. He didn't know much about the latest addition to their team, but he knew he liked her. His rapid-fire questions had debunked his theory that Katrina might be a fellow angel. Even still, he had a hunch that it was more than the planet Saturn that had brought her.

"I must ask Gabriel about her," he said to himself as he finished his latte with a final flick of the wrist. In the end, his leaf design looked more like corn on the cob, but it was certainly an improvement on the ghostly blob floating in yesterday morning's latte.

Manny had come to love these quiet mornings in the café. Not many employees would enjoy the extra responsibility, but when Chelsea asked if he would take on early-morning prep so she could have more time with the kids, he had jumped at the chance. (And he even landed on his feet.)

Ever since the God Blog went live, the café had been a hub of constant activity. But as much as Manny enjoyed the rush of customers, he relished more his moments in Grandmother Sophia's prayer closet.

He followed a trail of whispers to a set of doors tucked between the staircase and the café. He pulled back the accordion doors, drinking in the sights and sounds of a sunroom washed in buttery paint and brimming with boxes, antiques, and trinkets from eras past. Delicate lace drapes framed a picture-perfect bay window, still hours away from flooding the room with light. Nestled between the floaty antique fabric was a wingback chair holding a needlepoint pillow with the phrase *Living on coffee and a prayer.* Manny sipped his latte and leaned into the space. The whispers swelled into words and phrases pulled from the ether. He closed his eyes and listened to the symphony . . . the kind only angels hear.

"Oh Father, you are faithful and true . . ."

"I need your help, God . . ."

". . . bring healing to my family"

"Lord, bless my daughters . . ."

Decades of prayers resounded through the small room. Prayers that pass through the lips in a moment, but endure for all eternity.

". . . help my girls to forgive their father . . ."

". . . thank you for your mercy . . ."

"Lord, give Chelsea the grace she needs . . ."

"May your angels be encamped around my family . . ."

". . . and let this place be a house of prayer."

As Manny soaked in the chorus of prayers, his eyes roamed the maze of memories that filled the room. Beneath the film of dust was a colorful past. Stacks of photo albums, a rainbow of books, newspaper clippings. In the far corner, an imposing cabinet showcased rows of amber and green Depression glass dotted with blue ribbons and elementary school pottery projects. To Manny's right, a mint-condition phonograph sat atop a tower of vinyl records, surrounded by several hand-loomed tapestries and a small rocking horse from Mexico.

Remembering the family's vacation in Acapulco brought a smile to Manny's face. He could still see a carefree Chelsea splashing through the waves on the beach, one hand in her mom's, the other tucked securely in her dad's. Manny had been with

Chelsea through it all. Yet for all the progress she had made, Chelsea still had a lot of unpacking to do.

Manny pulled the doors shut. As he did, an image flashed before him. A vision of the room from heaven's view. Cutting through the dark landscape of the neighborhood, a glow had been emanating from this very corner of the café. Manny was certain this forgotten corner was meant to be more than a storehouse for memories; it was a sacred space. A house of prayer. Though neglected for a time, Manny had a suspicion the room would soon be put to good use once again.

CHAPTER 20

"Mornin', Manny! Have you seen —" But the sight of Manny in a decorative Christmas cardigan seemed to grab the words right out of Chelsea's mouth. The pockets were decked with jingle bells and embroidered holly, and the buttons running up the center were cleverly disguised as ornaments adorning a Christmas tree of yarn. The very top button was a shiny star.

"Good morning, Chelsea! Have I seen what?" Manny walked down the hall, jingling all the way.

"Um . . . Have you seen . . . my cell phone. Yes, my cell phone! That's what I'm looking for." Chelsea busied herself looking around the café, stifling an eruption of laughter.

"Still missing? I will keep my eyes open!"

"If it doesn't turn up soon, I'll have to break down and get a new one. Not that I mind the reprieve." Chelsea tied an apron around her waist, preparing herself for the onslaught of morning customers already gathered outside the front door. "Don't these people want to sleep in? It's Saturday! And spring break no less!"

"Chelsea, have you thought about expanding?" Manny ventured.

"Expanding?"

Manny pointed to the room between the stairway and the café. Chelsea peeked through the door and smiled, her mind filling with happy memories. When her Grandmother Sophia opened the café, "the parlor," as she called it, offered a peaceful respite for patrons to read and study. Chelsea's mother had loved the windowed room so much she kept it for herself.

"Mom turned this into her prayer closet. It is a lovely space, isn't it?"

"You could seat ten or fifteen people in there."

With some organizing and a fresh coat of paint, Chelsea could imagine the room filled with customers, maybe even attracting new ones. But planning for the future would have to wait for the moment. Her existing customers were knocking on the front door.

Weekend mornings weren't typically busy, but this Saturday was proving to be the exception. Word about the blog was spreading, and visitors were driving from miles away to claim a seat in the café and post their questions. They came from Dallas, Austin, and the Rio Grande Valley. Of late, they were also driving from Santa Fe, Little Rock, and even Tulsa.

Thankfully, Manny was always there, and Katrina was but a phone call away. Chelsea's extra help could not have come at a better time. The two were a dynamic duo. Manny brought warmth and personality; Katrina brought experience and technique. In fact, Katrina's arrival at the café had sparked its own wave of new customers, coffee connoisseurs who relished the artisan experience. Judging by the influx of Café Cosmos signature tumblers, Katrina's converts were many. It was safe to say the Higher Grounds Café was giving the nearest franchise a run for its money.

Chelsea slipped back upstairs to enjoy a family breakfast. Hancock had the makings of a great chef, and Emily proved to be an accomplished taste tester. Together they had whipped up a family favorite: cinnamon pecan pancakes. The kitchen smelled like Christmas morning. Or maybe that was just Chelsea, who had been feeling rather festive ever since her run-in with Manny.

"That's not really what you're wearing for the day, is it, Mom?" Hancock asked as they made their way downstairs to face the crowd.

The question caught Chelsea off guard. "Um . . ." She glanced down at her outfit. Maybe the purple Crocs were a mistake, but the jeans and black T-shirt didn't seem too offensive. "Is it really so bad?"

"Well . . ." Hancock's face twisted into an unsavory expression.

Chelsea turned to ask her two employees for their thoughts but stopped short at the site of Katrina in her plaid miniskirt, striped shirt, and knee-high combat boots and Manny dressed like, well, Santa's helper.

"It just makes you look old is all," Hancock said.

Moments later, Chelsea returned to the café in tailored khakis and a breezy chambray blouse. She knew her navy Converse lace-ups were only a half step up from the purple Crocs, but she hoped they exuded a youthful vibe.

"I guess that'll work," Hancock said as he and Emily darted back upstairs to watch cartoons.

Since when had her son become the fashion police? But a moment later, Chelsea was grateful for his intervention.

"*Konichiwa,* Mrs. Chambers." A young Japanese interpreter spoke for a dignified Japanese businessman. He handed Chelsea a box wrapped in decorative floral paper. "On behalf of my employer, Mr. Takeda, please receive this sincere gift."

"Um, hello." Chelsea took the package and dipped her head, hoping that was the appropriate gesture. "And . . . thank you. What brings you to the Higher Grounds Café?"

"Mr. Takeda came to your café in search of wisdom. To make inquiries of your blog from God."

"Well, I wouldn't call it mine . . ."

But Chelsea's humble explanation was interrupted by the motormouthed Mr. Takeda. His translator struggled to keep pace. "Thank you! Thank you for everything! Your café is a precious gift from heaven. For years my doubts and questions have overwhelmed me, but God knew. Today, I am free of my burden!"

As Mr. Takeda and his associate exited the café, Chelsea mirrored his bows and smiles, still hoping this was a culturally acceptable response. She couldn't imagine what the curious man had asked the God Blog, but she couldn't deny the sincerity of his gratitude. Nor the thousand dollars he left in the tip jar.

Curiosity got the best of her. With her phone still missing, Chelsea used Katrina's cell to scan the God Blog, all the while sipping from her new delicate Japanese mug.

"You've got to be kidding me," Katrina said with a surprising amount of inflection.

Chelsea and Katrina stared in wonder at the cell phone screen. Mr. Takeda's question was illegible. To them. The entire entry was in Japanese characters. And the kicker: so was the response. Chelsea marveled at the unlikelihood of it all. The café, this mysterious blog, her patrons from Arkansas, Oklahoma, and now Japan. "You know, I don't think this day could get any stranger."

Chelsea had spoken a moment too soon.

"Hey there, pretty lady."

She looked up to see Sawyer. In her café.

CHAPTER 21

"Beautiful day out there, huh?" Sawyer asked.

The weather? Why is he talking about the weather? Why is he even here?

There were so many things Chelsea could say to Sawyer in this moment, but nowhere on that list was today's chance of precipitation.

"Katrina, could you man the register, please? We'll just be a second."

As Chelsea led Sawyer to a quiet corner of the café, she noticed that a hush had fallen over the room. In her periphery she observed cell phones and tablets rising into the air as if gravity had lost its sway. Of course it had. The Sawyer Chambers show had entered the building. *Snap. Click. Ching.* Her patrons had become paparazzi. The very cell phones and tablets that moments ago were posting questions to God were now broadcasting this moment to the universe.

Chelsea leaned into Sawyer and spoke in sharp staccato whispers. "I'm sorry, have I missed something? We haven't spoken in weeks, and you come marching in like we're jolly old chums?"

Jolly old chums? Who even says that? Get it together, Chelsea, you're on Candid Camera.

"But I thought —"

"You thought what?"

Sawyer's brow crinkled unevenly like a confused puppy. Chelsea hated that expression. As if one adorable little gesture could absolve him of all guilt.

Not today.

Chelsea had rules, and he was breaking them. Or worse, acting like he had forgotten them. But Chelsea had not.

"Here you are." Manny approached the table with a latte in either hand. Chelsea noticed he had made the regrettable decision to fold his apron over and down, as if the Christmas tree on his sweater required more sunshine and open air. "One for you. And one for you." The bells on his sweater cuff jingled.

"Thank you, but this isn't necessary. Mr. Chambers was just leaving," Chelsea said.

But Manny was already gone.

"Would you look at that," Sawyer said.

Chelsea glanced at her latte to see what appeared to be Manny's attempt at coffee foam art. Was that a heart? Chelsea scrambled the shape with her spoon.

"So what's up with the Elf on the Shelf?" Sawyer joked.

"His name is Manny. And he's wonderful."

"Sure. Look, Chels, I was doing a job interview nearby, so when I got that last text —"

"A job interview? Nearby?" Chelsea was getting claustrophobic.

"Excuse me?" Another interruption. This time from a curvy soccer mom.

"How can I help you?" Chelsea asked.

But the woman brushed right past Chelsea. "Could I get your autograph?"

"Why, of course you can." Sawyer flashed his piano keyboard smile. "What's your name?"

"Jessica," she giggled. She handed Sawyer a slip of paper. Chelsea couldn't help but notice she wasn't wearing a wedding ring.

"You a football fan, Jessica?"

"Why, of course! Do you think we could get a picture together?" Her every syllable flirted.

"I don't see why not."

Jessica squealed. Chelsea crossed her arms and began tapping her foot against the wood floor.

"Would you mind?" Jessica passed her smartphone to Chelsea.

"Goodness, no! Why would I mind? This is fun, just so much fun."

Jessica clung to Sawyer as if she had just won *The Bachelorette.* No doubt she intended to share the image with everyone she knew.

"What a great photo this will be!" Chelsea said as she intentionally snapped a picture of her own index finger.

But Jessica didn't notice. She was too preoccupied with her next task: scribbling her phone number on a napkin and slipping it into Sawyer's jacket pocket.

As Jessica giggled her way out the door, Sawyer looked at Chelsea and shrugged. "Watcha gonna do? Anyway . . . so since I was nearby, I thought maybe after family fun day I could help you out at the café."

"Help me out?"

"Yeah."

For thirteen years Chelsea had orbited Planet Sawyer. Breaking free of his gravitational field would not be easy. Like a rocket ship leaving earth, such a journey would require decisive action, serious momentum, and focused thrust in a single direction. But Chelsea was ready to fly.

She stood up and stared Sawyer straight in the eye. "Thank you, but I don't need your help." She turned on her heel and marched back to the café counter.

But Sawyer flew close behind, chasing her through a crowd of customers. "Yeah, sure. I've been hearing good stuff. The whole blog thing . . . I'm not surprised."

"Not surprised?"

"Chelsea Hancock always has the answers."

"Ha!" Chelsea's laughter came out louder than intended. Not all the answers, apparently. Finally! A question worthy of the God Blog: *Dear God, how do I make my hopefully-soon-to-be-ex-husband go away?*

"You know what, Sawyer? You probably wouldn't believe just how wonderful things are going for the Higher Grounds Café. And for me!" Chelsea stood nose to nose with her husband. "Everyone loves my cupcake recipes. And have you met Katrina? She is a fabulous coffee artist. She's like a regular Lamborghini! What am I saying? That's a car. Katrina is a regular Leonardo da Vinci. Say hi, Katrina!"

"Hi, Katrina," Katrina said, slowly backing into the kitchen.

"And this guy, just look at him!" Chelsea slipped behind the counter, continuing the tour of her incredible new life. She placed an arm around Manny. "There is simply no end to his talents! He sweeps. He bakes. He performs miracles. With a twist of the wrist he fixed Mom's broken espresso machine. I mean, can you believe it?"

"That's, um . . . really impressive," Sawyer said.

"It's nothing, really. I was just trying to help."

Chelsea burst into laughter. "Oh, Manny, don't be so modest!" Chelsea turned to face Manny square on. "You should never sell yourself short like that. You're a very important member of this team, and I am overwhelmed with gratitude. I really just don't know what to say!"

Chelsea leaned in and planted a big kiss on Manny, then turned to face Sawyer again.

"Excuse me." Manny stumbled into the kitchen, head down, sweater jingling.

"Wow," Sawyer said. His wide eyes were fixed on Chelsea, who was now steadying herself on the counter and gasping for air.

"Daddy!" Hancock and Emily rushed

downstairs. Sawyer scooped them into his arms.

Chelsea whimpered, hoping her children hadn't witnessed her momentary lapse of sanity.

"You made it!" Hancock said.

"Of course I did, buddy."

Something didn't feel quite right to Chelsea. "I'm sorry . . . I'm still not clear. Why is it you came?"

"Because . . ." Sawyer tiptoed through a minefield. "You invited me to family fun day . . . at the Scobee Planetarium?"

Chelsea's confused expression confused Sawyer all the more.

"You just texted me this morning . . . told me to bring presents for the kids. Are you okay?"

"I never texted you," Chelsea said to Sawyer while her eyes drilled into her son.

"I'll show you." Sawyer dug through his pockets for his cell phone.

"Don't bother. Hancock, give me back my phone."

Hancock lowered his eyes and slowly pulled the phone from his back pocket.

Painful realization washed over Sawyer. "Chels, I'm sorry. I shoulda known."

"No, no. This is between Hancock and me. Come with me, young man." Chelsea all but dragged her son to the landing of the stairs. "Hancock, why would you take my phone without permission?"

"Why? Because I wanted to see Dad, and I knew you'd just say no."

Chelsea was stuck, and she knew it. Refuse Hancock time with his father, and risk losing his affection. Consent, and risk losing control.

"So can I go with Dad or not?"

Chelsea exerted what little power she had left. "You're not going anywhere in that outfit. Change first, and make sure to grab a jacket."

She returned to the café to find Sawyer and Emily sitting across from one another at a dainty tea table. Sawyer's sprawling athletic frame overwhelmed the decorative parlor chair, while little Emily, barely managing to keep her head above the table, hung onto her father's every word. There was no denying Sawyer's presence was magnetic. When he spoke, people leaned in — or in Emily's case, looked up.

"Please have them back for dinner," Chelsea said, though she couldn't bring her eyes to meet Sawyer's.

"Sure thing. We can grab lunch on our way there, if that's —"

But Chelsea had already disappeared upstairs.

CHAPTER 22

Chelsea was crouched in a small, dark corner of her room. She needed a moment alone. She needed to breathe. She needed to apologize to Manny. She needed to create a numerical password for her cell phone.

She stared at the little black device in her palm. Amazing how one little thing could cause so much trouble. Before braving her way through the security settings, she scanned the text messages Hancock had sent to Sawyer posing as her.

WHERE ARE YOU?

NOT TOO FAR AWAY ACTUALLY. ON A JOB INTERVIEW. WOULD LOVE TO TELL YOU ABOUT IT. BUT DON'T WANT TO BREAK ANY RULES.

YOU SHOULD COME BY THE CAFÉ TOMORROW! THE KIDS WOULD LOVE TO SEE YOU.

R U SERIOUS?

YES. FAMILY FUN DAY. YOU SHOULD

TAKE THE KIDS OUT FOR PIZZA AND THEN
THE PLANETARIUM.

OF COURSE. I CAN'T WAIT!

ME TOO.

WHAT R U WEARING? ;-)

PRETTY CLOTHES. MAKE SURE TO BRING
GIFTS FOR THE KIDS.

At least Hancock's unusual behavior that
morning made sense. Still, Chelsea cringed
at the thought of Hancock answering such
personal questions.

At least they didn't get any more personal
than that!

CHAPTER 23

"Mom, when is Dad going to live with us again?" Emily asked. "Yeah, Mom. When?" Hancock echoed from the top bunk.

Chelsea flipped the switch on Emily's new night-light.

"Oh, we'll have to talk about that. Later."

Chelsea had known this conversation was coming. But she had to have it with Sawyer first.

CAN YOU MEET ME AT THE CAFÉ?

Chelsea sent the text before she could talk herself out of it. Sawyer's response was almost immediate.

I'LL BE THERE IN HALF AN HOUR. IF U CAN PROVE THIS ISN'T HANCOCK. :)

Chelsea didn't know if she was ready to face Sawyer with the final verdict on their trial separation, but she was certainly well researched. *Be calm. Be direct. Be rehearsed.* She recited the tips to herself as she typed her response.

THANKS. SEE YOU THEN.

So far she was sticking with the script.

Chelsea saw the evening playing out as follows: Bo would come over and keep an eye on the kids while Chelsea and Sawyer had their talk. (She wanted to get out of the café in case things got heated.) She would lay out all of Sawyer's problems; he would get defensive. She would offer her solution; he would hopefully give his consent. End marriage. End scene.

"Are you sure I can't get you anything else, Bo?"

Chelsea placed a glass of water on the table next to Bo, who was settling into the mahogany leather recliner in her living room.

"No, no. I've got a good book to read." He spread a heavy black Bible on his lap. The print was so large Chelsea could have read it from across the room. Still, he pulled a pair of thick reading glasses from the pocket of his shirt.

"Well, you're a saint. Thank you so much for coming," she said. "I hate to leave the kids alone late at night. I love all the traffic we've been getting these days, but you never know who'll be coming through your door."

"That's wise. I'm just happy to be a good

neighbor."

Chelsea's phone dinged, and her heart started beating double time. "All right, looks like my ride's here. I'll be back by curfew."

"Take your time," Bo said with a smile. "Bet you and your husband have a lot of catching up to do."

"Oh, I really shouldn't be long," Chelsea said, hoping it was true.

Chelsea and Sawyer walked side by side beneath a canopy of stars, but the two were light-years apart. Chelsea had suggested a sidewalk stroll through the neighborhood.

Sawyer agreed. "Great way to start the evening."

And a great way to end it, Chelsea said to herself.

"Did you know they think there are more than a septillion stars? That's a one with twenty-four zeros behind it." Sawyer's neck was craned toward the heavens as he recounted his findings from the planetarium. "I can't even wrap my mind around it."

Calm. Direct. Rehearsed.

"Sawyer . . ." Chelsea stopped beneath a streetlamp and drew a deep breath. "I want a divorce."

Sawyer stopped and exhaled, his large frame shrinking before Chelsea's eyes.

"Chelsea . . . please . . ." he sputtered in a pained whisper.

His reaction took her off guard.

"I, uh . . ." She struggled to remember the next line in her script. "I have every reason, Sawyer. You put us all at risk. You lied, cheated, lost our money, and acted with utter disregard for your family. You were supposed to be the one protecting us. And I can't think of anyone who has done us more harm."

Chelsea was breathless by the time she finished her speech. She paused, bracing herself for Sawyer's usual sidestepping and deflecting.

"You're right," he said.

"What?"

Sawyer looked his wife square in the eye. "You're right. You said all the things I should have said. It's not easy to hear. But it's a fraction of what you lived through."

Sawyer's admission disarmed her. She hardly recognized this version of her husband.

"Chelsea, I can't take back the things I've done, and it's time I start owning my actions. Believe me, if that blog of yours had a delete button for regrets, I'd use it in a heartbeat."

"You and me both," Chelsea said. "Who

knows? Maybe it'll be in the upgrade."

Sawyer tried to smile, but his sadness wouldn't permit it. His lower lip pressed against his upper. His voice choked as he said, "You're a good person, Chelsea. And mom . . . and wife."

"Sawyer . . ."

"I know, I know. But it's true. I had all the ingredients of a great life, and I blew it. Why? Why did I do that?"

Chelsea had given up trying to answer that question months ago.

"Could we . . . is there any chance we could try again?" Sawyer said, taking a seat on a nearby bench. Chelsea eased herself down next to him.

Her silence was her answer.

Sawyer lifted his eyes to the stars. "I've got some questions I'd like to ask God."

"Don't we all?"

CHAPTER 24

Hancock lay wide awake counting the stars. The night-light Sawyer had given to Emily projected the Milky Way onto the walls and ceiling of their bedroom. After three attempts surpassing 500 stars, he lost track at 316 and called it quits. The constellations turning on the ceiling were no match for the questions turning in his head.

He peered down to the bottom bunk, where the lights twinkled across Emily's sleeping face. He eased himself down the ladder and crept across the room where the scintillating sphere revolved on a bookshelf. As he adjusted the dimmer, the stars swelled and then faded to black like a mass supernova.

"Cool," Hancock whispered, creating a series of stellar explosions before he tiptoed out of the room.

"Hi there, sleepwalker."

Hancock stopped at the threshold of the

kitchen. Bo stood at the stove pouring steaming water into a floral teacup. He wore his usual plaid shirt and carpenter jeans, but he had thick glasses balancing on the end of his nose and sheepskin slippers on his feet. The sight of Bo looking so at home in their kitchen was surprising and somehow comical.

"Your mom asked me to hang out here and keep an eye on things while she's out."

"That explains the glasses," Hancock said playfully. "But the shoes?"

Bo chuckled. "Well, you've got your wits about you. I take it you haven't been snoozing. Everything okay?"

"Just can't sleep." Hancock's head and shoulders slumped, as if he were struggling beneath an unseen burden.

"How about a cup of tea and some boring conversation?" Bo asked.

Hancock grinned. "That should do the trick."

The two settled with their teacups in the living room.

"I'm so tired." Hancock took a sip of his Sleepy Time tea.

"You want to go back to bed?"

"Oh no, I can't sleep. I'm just tired of . . . being mad. And sad. You know?"

Bo leaned forward, pulling his recliner

upright. "Rough day?"

"That's just it. I had a great day, and I still feel like this. I can't make myself stop." Hancock shifted in his seat, flicking at the tea bag in his mug. "I guess I'm just weird."

"No way," Bo said. "I've felt like that before. Couldn't make myself stop either."

"Then what did you do? You seem happy now." Hancock's eyes never left his mug.

"Did the only thing I knew to do," Bo said, reaching for the Bible on the end table. "There's an answer for every occasion in here. Like a map for life."

Hancock watched as Bo navigated the large book like a seasoned sailor.

"Here we are," the older man said, anchoring a page with his finger. "This is Jesus talking. He says, 'Come to Me, all of you who are weary and burdened, and I will give you rest.' "

Hancock looked up, his eyes glistening. His voice wavered beneath waves of emotion. "How does that work?"

CHAPTER 25

Manny was lost. Lost in a galaxy far, far away. He had been to three showings of *Star Wars* that week, and he managed to get lost on the way home every time. Always in a different direction. On this particular night he wandered six blocks into the Lavaca neighborhood before his mind emerged from deep space.

"Uh-oh," he whispered upon discovering he had no idea where he was. Again. Fortunately, Manny always had a map on hand. All he had to do was look up.

"Amazing!" Manny marveled as he plopped onto a nearby bench, scanning the night sky for the Big Dipper. He traced the saucepan with his finger and followed the trail to the one star he could always count on. "Gotcha!" He pinched the North Star between his thumb and forefinger, then stood up, getting his bearings.

"You might not want to leave just yet."

Manny could feel the hot white light of an angelic presence blazing behind him. "Gabriel!" he exclaimed.

"What'd you call me?" A gruff voice ripped through the air.

Manny's eyes darted across the street to a hulkish figure swaggering to the curb. He had the wide shoulders of a wrestler and the snarl of a jackal. He glared at Manny from beneath a hoodie. "What are you doing on my street?"

Gabriel intervened. "Enough with you!"

The figure didn't challenge. He turned and disappeared.

Gabriel chuckled. "Don't worry, I've got your back."

"And don't come back!" Manny shouted across the street. He pivoted on his heels to face Gabriel. "Am I glad to see you." He blinked through the blinding brightness. He could feel his pupils shrinking. "I have so many questions."

"And I have answers. But first there's something you need to see." Gabriel grasped Manny's shoulder. The street faded away and a room began to form around them. He could still feel the concrete beneath his feet, but when he looked down he saw an oriental rug and distressed wood floors. What he saw when he lifted his eyes nearly knocked him off his feet.

Angels everywhere. Shoulder to shoulder, they filled the upper level of the Higher Grounds Café, creating a halo of light. At the center of the circle, Hancock and Bo sat side by side, heads bowed in prayer, unaware of their enraptured audience.

The reverence in the room was tangible. The angels knew this moment for what it was. Holy and sacred. A heart was opening itself for the greatest gift of the universe, the presence of God.

But through the window, Manny noticed dark shadows lurking. A wind whistled into the room, and a dark cloud serpentined around Hancock, its tendrils reaching and grasping at the young boy. Voices emerged from within: throaty and gutteral, filling the atmosphere with lies of shame, abandonment, and despair.

"God has no place for you, Hancock."

"God? What God?"

Just as the corruptive fog drifted toward Hancock's consciousness, Gabriel began to sing. "Holy is the Living God."

At the sound of the angelic voice, the murky cloud stopped its advance.

"Blessed be the name of the Lord! Blessed be the name of the Lord!"

The shadows inched back at each chorus.

One by one the angels joined Gabriel, lifting their voices to heaven. It soon sounded as though hundreds, perhaps thousands were singing. Outside the window, multitudes of angels orbited the house, bathing it with song. In the presence of such mighty voices, the evil encircling Hancock held no sway. There was no shadow for such lies to hide.

Manny laughed as the abysmal cloud dissolved into the air. "Resist the Devil and he will flee from you," he quoted as he stood next to the much taller Gabriel.

"Thy kingdom come! Thy will be done!" Gabriel invited.

Manny sang along with the chorus of angels. What he lacked in tone he made up for in volume as he beckoned to the Father.

Then it happened. A descent of light straight from heaven's throne, a ball aflame with glory and color. It was sunrise, sunset, silver, and golden. It was every color of the rainbow. A thousand and one hues. Vibrant like a star, gentle as a candle flicker, it hovered over the boy and then entered his spirit.

The angels pronounced the victory:

"Chosen by God!"

"Redeemed for eternity!"

"Full of God's Spirit!"

"Forever forgiven!"

"Born anew!"

Light surged through the cracks and crevices, not just mending but recreating Hancock's innermost being.

The chorus of angels erupted with a new verse. "Holy, holy, holy is the Lord God Almighty!"

Manny was still singing when Gabriel lifted his hand from his shoulder, drawing him back to the present. It was hard to believe his feet had never left the pavement. "Thank you," he whispered, first in a prayer, then to Gabriel. "Witnessing that. Each time it is stunning. But this time, with Hancock . . . he is a special boy."

"Special indeed. And you played a part in changing his life," Gabriel said. "You're doing great work down here, Manny."

"You really think so? 'Cause today . . . today was rough."

"But you rose to the occasion. Took that kiss like a man."

"You saw that?" Manny's ears started to feel hot. "I mean, of course you did. You just wouldn't believe how confusing things get down here. So many details, so many people, so many emotions!"

"It all seems a little simpler from heaven's view," Gabriel agreed.

"Of course, the humans do have a few perks. Have you seen *Star Wars*?"

Gabriel nodded. "Seen all of them."

Manny startled. "Wait. There's more than one?"

"Oh yeah. There are a bunch. But the first three are best."

Manny was jittery with excitement. "Could this night get any better?"

CHAPTER 26

"I've missed this, Chelsea. We're good at this."

Chelsea stood on her front porch, studying Sawyer's face. She could tell he was sincere. Detached from reality maybe, but entirely earnest.

"Good at what? Talking? Strolling beneath the stars? This isn't real life."

Sawyer took a step back. Chelsea knew her response had shocked him, and all she could do was shake her head.

"We *can* do real life," he answered. "The good, the bad, the ugly. I mean, how much uglier can it get?"

"I don't plan to find out!"

Sawyer reached for Chelsea's hand. "I know we can do this, Chelsea. We can make it. Together."

The words ripped open the space-time continuum. Chelsea was sitting on the bed of her dorm room, looking into the same big blue eyes filled with hope and determination. Sawyer had no idea he was repeating history, but she would never forget. Chelsea couldn't alter the past, but this was her chance to change the future.

"I have every reason I need to divorce you."

"I know you do," Sawyer conceded, pain gleaming in his eyes. "But I'm going to keep hoping you don't."

Just before going upstairs, Chelsea took one last look out the window. What she saw didn't surprise or disappoint her. Not anymore. She'd lived through this before. Sawyer, phone to his ear, calling someone well after midnight.

Every reason indeed.

Like an overworked computer, Chelsea's mind struggled to process all the events of the day. She had almost forgotten Bo was waiting upstairs.

"Well, how were they?" Chelsea asked.

"Perfect little angels," Bo said. "I had a good chat with Hancock."

"Oh?"

"I'll let him fill you in." Bo grinned. "And you? How was your night?"

Chelsea was far too weary to put on a show. "Fine. We're getting a divorce. But it's for the best. Sawyer is great on holidays.

But real life? Not so much."

"Sounds an awful lot like my wife's first husband."

"Oh yeah?"

"She was married to a drunk. Arrested twice for DUI. Had trouble making it to work. A real deadbeat dad. He made excuses to go on 'business trips' just so he could drink and party."

"Good thing she left him."

"She never did, actually. She kicked him out all right, but he kept coming back like a bad penny."

"Sounds familiar. So how'd she finally get rid of him? I could use some tips."

"Well, to be honest, you're looking at him."

Chelsea stared long and hard at her neighbor. "That was you? What happened?"

"Hard to say without sounding trite. But you see, God . . ." Bo scratched his chin, searching for the right words. "Well, I guess he came after us. Really pursued us. Through friends. Through events. Even through our rotten marriage. I wanted a better wife. She wanted a better husband. But God gave us something even better. Himself." Bo stared off into space, his eyes welling with tears. "Joanne and I were together forty years. I do miss her."

"I'm so sorry," Chelsea said.

Bo collected his Bible and coat and stood to go. Then he turned and looked directly at her. "Your mother once asked me to pray for you and Sawyer. I want you to know I haven't stopped."

"I don't think it'll ever work out between us, Bo."

"Maybe, maybe not. Not really my business, I reckon. Either way, I think you should know . . . God's pursuing you, Chelsea."

CHAPTER 27

"What's the year?" Sara pulled a vintage photo from the album on her lap for Chelsea to see. The image showed a much younger Sara in the middle of a science experiment, complete with a lab coat and goggles. The hairstyles and fashions around her screamed nineteen eightysomething.

Chelsea scanned the image for a clue. Noticeably absent was the hairline scar on Sara's chin, but that could be anytime before 1990. It didn't help that Sara had the same long, silky blond curls until she turned thirty. Then Chelsea got it. "Oh! Fall 1989."

"That's seven for seven!" Sara said, checking Chelsea's answer against the date on the back. "How'd you know this time?"

"Elementary, my dear. See that kid behind you? That's Roger Halbrook. He was in your chemistry class the first half of your freshman year. Deb had a crush on him."

"You guys were in fourth grade!"

"You know Deb. She always had a thing for older guys."

"Now that we've confirmed you're the next Sherlock Holmes, I'll get back to work." Sara began tucking the photos back into their respective places in the album. "I just needed a brain break."

"I'm sorry, Sara. You're the one moving, and here I am asking you to help me pack up. But we're making progress. Watch this!" Chelsea glided from one side of the sunroom to the other. After three consecutive evenings working through the cluttered maze, this was a considerable feat.

Sara offered a small smile.

"Everything okay?" Chelsea asked.

"Well, I didn't want to burden you, but the offer fell through on the house. The For Sale sign goes back up on Monday."

"I'm so sorry, Sara. You could've told me."

"Don't worry about it. But at this rate we'll be in a new school district just in time for the twins to start kindergarten."

"Any more boxes, Mom?" Hancock stood in the doorway.

"Um, that stack by the phonograph goes home with Aunt Sara. Everything else can be stored in here." Chelsea gestured to the apothecary cabinet she and Sara had centered on the wall. "We're down to three boxes!"

"Want me to take your stuff to the car?" Hancock asked.

"That'd be great! Thank you, sir," Sara said.

Hancock stacked several books on a cardboard box, bracing the tower with his chin.

"You're amazing!" Chelsea called to him as he continued his balancing act down the hall.

"He seems to be in good spirits," Sara said once he was out of earshot.

Chelsea smiled thoughtfully. "He really does. He told me he had a great talk with Bo the other night. Didn't say too much, but he's clearly feeling a lot better. And I sure can tell a difference."

"I'm glad Hancock's spending time with Bo, and I bet Bo loves the company. His only son is stationed overseas, so they don't see each other much."

"Oh, that has to be hard on him," Chelsea said. She opened one of the last boxes. "More photo albums to go through! Could you imagine if Mom had had a Facebook account?"

Sara shook her head. "There's one plus side to her resistance to technology!"

"Seriously," Chelsea said, flipping past a

series of brace-faced photos from her awkward phase. She lifted up one snapshot and gazed at it. Ten-year-old Chelsea at a costume party, wearing her mom's oversized, polka dot dress, yellow Easter hat, and high heels stuffed with tissue paper. She was blowing a kiss to the camera.

Chelsea smiled, remembering her mom on the other side of the lens. "Like this, sweetie!" Virginia had said, coaxing her daughter into the playful pose. Chelsea did her best impression. "Perfect!"

Chelsea had wanted to be just like her mom when she grew up. She thought her mother really was perfect. Now she knew otherwise. "You know, I had a hard time at first reconciling how Mom could end up in such a bad place financially and not tell anyone. But after walking in her shoes for a few months, I kind of get it. Running a business is hard, and sometimes admitting you need help is even harder."

Sara nodded, but Chelsea could tell her mind was elsewhere, lost in a memory of her own. "What do you have?" Chelsea asked, scooting over to join her sister.

Sara was studying an image of herself in a hospital bed. Little Chelsea stood beside her with a somber smile. Sara's face was bruised and swollen. One eye was completely closed. A line of stitches ran from the left corner of her mouth to her jaw.

Chelsea shuddered. The girls had been spending a typical weekend with their father. He was away on a "business trip" on a Saturday night, leaving sixteen-year-old Sara to look after eleven-year-old Chelsea. Chelsea had awakened trembling and choking after a nightmare. She saw shadows in the windows, menacing shapes on the walls of her makeshift bedroom. Faceless creatures circled her bed, grasping at her throat. The same vivid dream that had haunted her over the years.

Chelsea had begged Sara to take her back to their mom, and that was the last thing she remembered. The rest of her "memory" came from an article that ran in the *Tribune*. The girls had been struck by a drunk driver just after Sara merged onto the highway. An eyewitness saw the little blue Volkswagen flip three times before landing on its side in a cloud of smoke and flames. When the paramedics and fire fighters arrived at the scene, Chelsea and Sara had been rescued from the fiery wreck by a Good Samaritan stranger. Chelsea made it out unscathed. Sara's recovery was long and hard.

"You want to know something weird?" Sara asked, unconsciously tracing the scar on her face. "I'm thankful for the whole thing."

Chelsea remained silent. Who was she to argue with Sara? Her sister wore a constant reminder of the traumatic event. Yet deep within herself, Chelsea felt a wound that had gone untreated. A wound still stinging with doubt, fear, and regret.

"That experience opened my eyes to how deep God's love is. I'm reminded of his love for me every time I look in the mirror."

"You're just so certain about it," Chelsea marveled. "I have the hardest time believing that the God of the universe watches over me and you. The idea that he loves us individually. It sounds nice. But it also sounds like a fairy tale."

"I know God was watching over us that night, Chelsea."

"Then why did we get in the accident in the first place?"

Sara paused before answering, slowly assembling her thoughts, or perhaps working up the courage to share them. "Personally? I think there's more going on around us than we realize. I think God uses even the bad and ugly things in this world to lead us to a good place."

"You sound like Mom," Chelsea said, pulling herself to her feet and bringing the conversation to a close. "Hey, did you ever find her Sinatra album? I've had that 'Lost in the Stars' song she loved stuck in my head, but I only know the chorus."

"We're lost in the stars, lost in the stars . . ." Sara chirped in an airy soprano. "That's all I know, but I love that song! I'm sure it's over there. Like a needle in a haystack," she added, motioning toward their mom's extensive record collection.

"Good thing the chorus is nice," Chelsea joked.

When she went upstairs for the night, Chelsea was still humming "Lost in the Stars." When she peered into Emily and Hancock's room, she found herself living the lyrics. Beneath the starry scape of their night-light, Hancock and Emily were kneeling at the foot of the bunk bed in prayer, their reverent murmurs indiscernible to Chelsea's ear. She had countless memories of being on bended knee in that very room. Each evening, Chelsea's mother led her in a nightly prayer, but tonight Hancock filled the role. Part of Chelsea wanted to step in and play her proper part, but since she wouldn't know where to begin, she quietly slipped away.

CHAPTER 28

"Sign is . . . bro-ken," Emily sounded out, her index finger tracing the letters of Faith Community Church's marquee. "M-mes —"

"Message," Chelsea assisted.

"Sign is broken. Message inside!"

"Very good, sweetie!" Chelsea laughed at Tony's wit and at Emily's display of academic skill.

"What does it mean?" Emily asked.

"It means Uncle Tony wants people to come inside the church to hear his sermon," Hancock said.

Today was a landmark Sunday for Faith Community Church. It was the fifth anniversary of the church's revitalization under the pastorship of Tony and Sara Morales. To mark the occasion, Tony custom-ordered three dozen cupcakes from Chelsea: chocolate espresso and vanilla latte. He'd been brewing a special coffee-themed message, and as his marquee implied, he wanted everyone to come inside to taste and see just how good it was going to be.

He even used coffee as a part of his sermon: "When you sip a cup of coffee and say, 'This is good,' what are you saying? The coffee beans are good? The coffee machine is good? The hot water? The filter?"

Tony paced up and down the center aisle, his eyes connecting with each member of his meager flock. As Tony hoped, his congregation of blue-hairs was savoring every word, and to Chelsea's surprise, so were her children. Emily giggled when her Uncle Tony waved to her as he passed.

" 'Good' happens when *all* the ingredients work together!" Tony approached a raised table, which displayed his sermon props: a bag of coffee, filters, a coffee maker, and a pitcher of water. "When the beans are roasted to perfection and ground into powder, when the water is heated to just the right temp, or if you're my sister-in-law, if the pressure is just right to pull a perfect shot of espresso . . . it's the collective co-operation of all these elements that creates *good.*"

Chelsea smiled politely as eyes darted in her direction, but her mind was drifting elsewhere. Someone somewhere was jingling keys. Chelsea looked toward the front row, where an elderly man sat on the other side of Sara. Chelsea sat up straight. The old man was her father.

Of course Sara would bring him to the anniversary service. But why was he being so rude? Had he developed some weird nervous tic?

From then on, Chelsea heard only the occasional phrase from Tony. "Is a famine or heart attack good? . . . the life of Joseph . . . struggle, storms, death . . . God works it all together . . ."

Tony's sermon culminated with an enticing sip of steaming, freshly brewed coffee, which was the perfect cue for Chelsea to escape into the lobby with Hancock and Emily. She busied herself behind the church's makeshift coffee counter, arranging her custom-flavored cupcakes and decanters of flavored coffee.

"You know my niece!" shouted a wheelchair-bound man in a stylish fedora and a tailored sport coat. The man was younger than most of his fellow churchgoers, and his athletic physique made him seem all the more out of place in a wheelchair.

"Do I?" Chelsea handed the man a vanilla

latte cupcake and a paper mug filled with coffee.

"Katrina!" His boisterous voice filled the foyer. "I'm sure glad she found your café. She can be a little hard around the edges."

"Well, my customers love her, and so do I."

"I'm sure you're a good influence on her too."

"I don't know about that," Chelsea said.

"My name is Frank, by the way. Work keeps me busy, but I hope to stop by the café soon. As a bona fide IT nerd, I'm itching to snoop around that network of yours."

Chelsea chuckled. "Please do! By the way, I'm Chel—" The sight of her father walking through the lobby stopped her short. The urge to quickly duck behind the counter and tie her shoe was overwhelming, and Chelsea envisioned the former version of herself doing just that — cowering and hiding, hoping her old man would just disappear. But new Chelsea stood straight, shook Frank's hand, and finished her sentence. "I'm Chelsea. Hope to see you at the café soon."

While Chelsea served the last of her church patrons, her father stood in a corner and watched, all the while jingling a set of keys. Chelsea created a mental Post-it note to ask Sara about his odd behavior. For a moment she even considered getting the answer from him firsthand. But that would require her to speak to him, which was out of the question. Looking back was no better than driving a car with her eyes glued to the rearview mirror. If Chelsea and her family were going to move forward, she had to stay focused on the road ahead.

She turned her attention back to her work.

CHAPTER 29

"So that website you got. You can ask it any question, and God answers back?" The scrawny young boy stared at Chelsea from across the counter.

Thankfully the weather had warmed since the last time Marcus was in. So had the boy's countenance, especially after hearing that God might be waiting on the other side of Chelsea's blog.

"Well . . ." Chelsea weighed her words. "That is what I hear. Although I've never tried it. How are you, Marcus?"

"I'm fine," the boy said as he counted every nickel and dime from his pockets.

"Your mom still drinking a triple breve?"

"Yeah, but how'd you know?" Marcus's eyes were half closed in suspicion.

"I have a knack for remembering things." Chelsea sighed. "Everything actually." She scooped up the boy's change without counting. "Aren't you supposed to be in school,

Marcus?"

"I homeschool," he said, casting his eyes to the floor. Now it was Chelsea's turn to be suspicious.

She handed Marcus the triple breve for his mom, a hot chocolate for him, and a few scones for the road. "These are on the house. You come and see me anytime, okay?"

"Wow, thanks, ma'am!"

As Marcus walked out the door, Chelsea was greeted by another familiar face.

"Deb! It's good to see you again! Just the other day, Sara and I found an old photo of your fourth-grade crush. Hilarious!"

Deb managed a slight smile. "Hi, Chelsea. It's lovely to see you." Deb exuded her usual posh vibe — tailored black dress, elegant silver jewelry, complementing accessories. "I love what you've done with the place."

"Thanks, Deb." Though Chelsea wondered how her old friend could see anything from beneath her thick designer sunglasses. "How have you been? Haven't seen you in a while."

"Oh, things have just been so busy, you know? I'd love a double shot of espresso and one of your mini scones."

As Manny and Katrina went to work on her order, Chelsea gambled a more sincere question. "You sure you're doing okay?"

"Oh . . ." Deb toyed with her wedding ring. "Do you think —"

"Delivery for Mrs. Chambers!" The arrival of a gigantic bouquet of yellow roses spoiled the moment.

"I can see you're doing well!" Deb said.

Chelsea rolled her eyes for dramatic effect. "If only my life were so rosy!" She put the bouquet aside and leaned toward Deb, hoping to continue their conversation. "Do I think what?"

"Do you think . . ." But the moment had passed. "Do you think I could use your Internet? I've been hearing some crazy things!"

"Of course. Anything you need."

While Deb secluded herself at a small tea table, Chelsea stole her own private moment in the nearly finished parlor. She plucked the note from the bouquet, then sat in her mother's old recliner to read it.

Are there any plans in the works for Hancock's birthday? Can't believe our boy is turning thirteen! P.S. Is this against the rules?

Chelsea tapped her fingers against the floral card stock. Was this against the rules?

174

She couldn't be sure. It occurred to her that as she moved forward with the divorce, she'd need to make lots of new rules. She had no idea where to start. For a passing moment she considered seeking advice from the God Blog. But she knew better. In fact, she could probably predict the answer. Wasn't it Jesus who said something about loving your enemies?

No thanks. Chelsea could write her own rule book for now.

"I don't even know what to ask. I've let my family down. I have so many secrets, and the guilt is killing me."

Chelsea listened as a sassy hipster read some of the sadder entries from the God Blog to a table of fellow hecklers. Ordinarily Chelsea didn't mind when her patrons read aloud from the blog. Plenty of people experienced a surge of hope and encouragement after visiting the site. But this mean-spirited intrusion struck a raw nerve with Chelsea.

After a bout of laughter, the girl continued with the answer.

"I know all your secrets, even the one tucked inside your wallet. If you only knew the gift I have for you and who you are speaking to, you would ask me, and I would give you living water. I would cleanse you from the inside out. I love you. I always have, and I always will. God"

Chelsea was glad the unfortunate entry didn't have a name associated with it. She scanned the café, wondering if the anonymous question had originated from her old friend. But Deb was no longer there.

CHAPTER 30

"Beautiful!" Manny exclaimed. "I can't wait to see this place filled with people tomorrow morning."

Chelsea took a step back to admire the sunroom, its transformation complete. The makeover managed to make the most of the small space while retaining its character and history, thanks to the apothecary cabinet, lace drapes, and antique wingback chair, not to mention the phonograph gleaming in the corner next to a tiered shelf lined with vintage records just begging to be played.

"Bo, you outdid yourself on these," Chelsea said, running a hand over one of two reclaimed wood tables running parallel with the wall.

"Don't forget my trusty sidekick!" Bo gave Hancock a slap on the back.

"Never!" Chelsea said, placing her flowers from Sawyer on one of the tables. "Hancock, have you thought about what you want to do for your birthday?"

"Yeah. I want to do what we always do," he said.

Chelsea bit her tongue. Sawyer and Hancock had an epic birthday tradition. A tradition that made Chelsea's knees quake and her stomach turn. Every year without fail, Sawyer would take Hancock to the nearest amusement park, where they would ride the tallest, fastest, loopiest roller coaster — one time for each year of Hancock's life. Chelsea, whose fear of heights topped her list of phobias, could not think of a worse way to celebrate a birthday. That is, until she added Sawyer to the equation.

"I was thinking we would start a new tradition this year. You know, now that you're going to be a teenager?" Chelsea attempted a positive spin, but she knew she had failed miserably before she even finished speaking. In fact, her tactic backfired.

"I know," Hancock said in a tone that reeked of teenage sarcasm. "Why don't you go ahead and plan my birthday? Then you can tell me what I want to do."

As soon as the words spurted out of his mouth he was gone, leaving Chelsea to ride the wake of awkward tension with Manny and Bo.

"What do you say we call it a night,

Manny?" Bo said.

Manny nodded. "Big day tomorrow!"

"Thanks, guys. You're the best. I better go have a chat with my son," Chelsea said. "Wish me luck," she added as she headed upstairs.

Chelsea found Hancock in the kitchen eating a bowl of ice cream. Her first instinct was to scold him for consuming sugar so late at night, but instead she served herself a scoop of Rocky Road and buckled up for a bumpy ride.

If you can't beat 'em, join 'em.

"Did everyone leave?" Hancock said after a moment of silence.

"Yeah. You probably owe Manny and Bo an apology tomorrow."

Hancock gave a heavy nod as he spooned at the chocolate puddle forming in his bowl. "It's hard, you know?"

Chelsea watched her son struggle to put his feelings into words, a hereditary trait no doubt.

"I don't like not being a family anymore," he said. "And every time I think I've gotten used to all the change, something else changes."

Chelsea's eyebrows rose with recognition. Her young son had pinpointed her exact feelings. She reached for his hand and gave it a reassuring squeeze.

"Mom, I know Dad's not perfect, and you don't want to see him. But he's my *dad*. You can't cut him out forever."

CHAPTER 31

Katrina pushed through the swinging door of the kitchen. "There's somebody here to see you."

"Does this person have a name?"

"Probably. I didn't get it though. He's tall. Smiles a lot. Looks a little like a GQ model."

Dennis Darling.

Chelsea smiled. "I'll be there in a few."

She had been cooking up a new recipe in her head, and with the added help in the café, she was enjoying the opportunity to actually make it. Chelsea didn't know how many layers this cake was going to have, and with the myriad of issues she had to process, it could very well turn into the Tower of Babel. But the cake could wait. Chelsea checked her reflection in the glass window of her shiny industrial oven and corraled a few stray hairs.

"Mr. Darling!" Chelsea stretched out her hand, but Dennis's hands were full.

"These are for you," he said, handing her two boxes of gourmet, oven-ready pizzas. "And the kids, of course."

"How incredibly thoughtful!"

"You're a hardworking woman. You deserve a break." There was that grin, the sparkling teeth, adorable dimple, rugged cleft. A feast for the eyes.

Chelsea couldn't think of a single intelligent thing to say, so she laughed, which struck her as even less intelligent than saying nothing at all. After a moment she managed a simple "Thanks."

"So, I was wondering —" Dennis started.

"Watch out!" Manny hollered as his wheeled mop bucket overturned, gushing mucky water over Mr. Darling's khaki slacks and suede lace-ups. "Whoops," Manny said, staring.

"I'm so sorry, Dennis!" Chelsea said.

"Please. Accidents happen."

"Manny, could you please grab a towel for Mr. Darling?"

"Yes, I will get a towel." Manny's tone lacked any sense of urgency, so too his leisurely stroll into the kitchen.

"Never mind." Chelsea grabbed a pile of napkins from the counter.

As the two attempted to rescue the soaking suede shoes, Dennis picked up where he left off. "I was wondering if we could have lunch together?"

"Oh?"

"If you're not too busy." That smile again.

After a quick wardrobe change, Chelsea stepped out of the café in a tailored black number she hadn't had any occasion to wear since her breakup with an NFL star.

"You've got kids?" Chelsea noted the scattered toys in the backseat of Mr. Darling's BMW SUV.

"Three of them. Most important part of my life."

"And you're not —"

"Nope. Divorced. Two years now."

"Sorry. I don't mean to pry."

"Don't worry. It was hard at first. I don't blame her any more than I blame myself. When it came to daily life, Suzanne and I just weren't suited for each other. It always felt like a battle with too many casualties. But now . . . The kids are doing great, and I really feel like I'm discovering myself again. Just me. It feels good."

"That's nice."

"Sorry. You weren't prying, and here I am gushing."

"No, no. It's good to hear, and I'm glad you're all doing so well. I'm actually in the middle of a similar situation."

"I kinda figured."

Their conversation continued to the patio of a quaint neighborhood bistro of Mr. Darling's choosing. Chelsea exhaled the stresses of her day, all the while drinking in the lovely sights and sounds of their surroundings. Trendy shoppers wandered in and out of equally trendy boutiques and restaurants, which just so happened to include Chelsea's main competition, Café Cosmos.

Dennis studied the wine list and ordered a bottle of something that sounded French and sophisticated.

"Two glasses?" he asked Chelsea.

"Why not?"

As the waiter left, Dennis resumed the questions. "So what's it been like, running your mom's old café?"

"Difficult, more than I imagined. It's a task, managing the café and this new version of our family. But there are moments when it is rewarding." Chelsea couldn't keep from smiling. "I know what you mean about discovering yourself again. It feels good being just me."

It also felt good sharing a meal and a conversation with someone other than a customer, coworker, or child.

By the time dessert was served, Dennis

was ready to cut to the chase.

"I'd like to buy the Higher Grounds Café."

"What?"

"I'd like to buy the Higher Grounds Café."

"Whatever for?"

Dennis pointed across the street. "In one month, the customer base of Café Cosmos has shrunk 40 percent. I should know. I'm one of the owners."

"Forty percent? Why so much?" Chelsea had a very good idea why that might be, but she wanted to hear it for herself.

"Because of your café. People love the artisan feel, the pastries, the coffee art, the vintage charm."

"The God Blog."

"Sure. But still, you're good at what you do."

"Suppose I were to sell the café to you. What then?"

"There's any number of scenarios. But I'll give you one. Run it for me. No tax burden to worry about. Let me shoulder the risk. You could manage it and sleep better at night."

Though Chelsea had been expecting to sell the property, she had never even considered selling her business. She'd never had the occasion. She could only guess at its selling price. Two hundred thousand? Three hundred? Five?

"One million sounds fair, don't you think?" she bluffed.

"One million sounds fair," Dennis replied without flinching.

Chelsea gulped her iced tea.

"Of course, in whatever scenario, the God Blog stays with the café," Dennis said.

"Of course. But you know it's not me pulling those strings."

"Then we hire whoever is. Or replace them. Your customers might not even know the difference. As I said, any number of scenarios. In the meantime, you do have a security system, right?"

"I guess I should, but I don't. The router is just tucked in a pantry next to the napkins and coffee beans."

"I wouldn't worry. My bigger point is this . . . Be wise. Protect yourself from anything or anyone who might be a taker, as I like to call them. I think Chelsea Chambers has a bright future ahead. An open road full of possibilities."

"I . . . Well . . . I dunno . . ."

Dennis gave Chelsea's hand a comforting squeeze. "A lot to think about, I know. I only hope you give this the consideration it deserves."

A future with possibilities. A million dollars. That luscious grin.

That night Chelsea baked into the wee hours, sorting her thoughts into luscious layers of cake. Espresso, crème brûlée, mocha, amandine . . .

Every scenario she considered seemed more delicious than the one before. She didn't know how many layers she would bake into this cake, but she couldn't wait to taste it.

CHAPTER 32

Petition for Dissolution of Marriage.

Chelsea studied the words, stiff and formal on the page, disconnected from the emotions and complexities they demanded. She slid the document back into the legal envelope, attempting the same art of detachment. Today was a day for celebrating. It was Hancock's birthday.

She thought back to the first time she'd held her son, with Sawyer by her side. She had never felt so accomplished, so full of hope. Today when she looked at Hancock, she felt the same. Only different. Chelsea felt as though she had reached the peak of a mountain, only to discover she had merely been climbing the foothills. There was a long way to go before she'd be looking down from a mountaintop.

Time to conqueror that fear of heights.

Chelsea crept upstairs with a confetti cupcake covered by a spiral of candles.

Thirteen, to be exact. She and Emily woke Hancock with the birthday song and blowing out of candles per the annual tradition. It was a family rule that on birthdays, dessert always came first. After a sweet appetizer, she and the kids walked to Hancock's favorite breakfast spot, leaving Manny and Katrina to hold down the fort, so they could enjoy a full day of celebration.

In previous years Hancock's birthdays had been full of over-the-top festivities. For his tenth birthday, Sawyer rented a jet and flew Hancock and his friends to opening day at Yankee Stadium before ending the night riding roller coasters on Coney Island. Sawyer was the king of 'extravagant surprises, but today Chelsea had one of her own in the works, albeit far humbler.

It was the perfect day to be outside. The spring air was just on the chilly side of perfect, and the birds seemed to be singing about it. The trio rented a horse-drawn carriage and told the driver to take his time. They moseyed through downtown San Antonio until they reached the Alamo.

Hancock loved the mission. Colonel Travis. Bowie. Crockett. Flashing sabres and blasting cannons — he loved every minute. Emily, on the other hand, got hungry.

Chelsea suggested the Pig Stand.

It was another San Antonio icon, a good old-fashioned American establishment that had been wooing local diners with its greasy-spoon appeal and kitschy decor since the 1920s. In the summers, the parking lot of the Pig Stand doubled as a doo-wop era dance floor in the evenings, but on this sunny spring day Chelsea entered the diner and enjoyed jukebox rock'n'roll.

Sara, Tony, and Bo were waiting for them at a vinyl-covered table complete with gifts and balloons. After a dozen hugs and "happy birthdays," Bo gave Hancock a set of tools and a navy leather Bible with his name on it. Sara and Tony gave him a special-edition set of the original *Star Wars* trilogy. Next came a round of "pig sandwiches" so tender and juicy they should have been served with bibs.

After lunch, Chelsea and the kids piled into Sara and Tony's van and set off for their next destination.

"No peeking!" Emily gleefully scolded her brother, who was tugging at the blindfold they had fastened around his head.

"Are we there yet?" Hancock asked.

"Gettin' closer!" Tony called from the driver's seat.

This conversation was repeated five more

times before the van pulled to a stop. Chelsea helped Hancock out of the car and led him about fifteen steps before a heavy rumbling followed by a distant wave of shrill screams and nervous laughter gave their location away.

"Fiesta Texas!" Hancock exclaimed, ripping the blindfold from his eyes.

The sprawling amusement park had been built into the side of an old rock quarry when Chelsea was a teenager.

"So, what do you think?" she asked as they approached.

"Awesome!" Hancock exclaimed. "Can we ride the Poltergeist?"

"You better believe we're going to ride it!"

"Dad!" Hancock zigzagged through a tour group from the Netherlands and into the arms of Sawyer.

"Happy Birthday! Surprised?"

Hancock nearly nodded his head off. "Totally! But how —" He looked over at his mom.

"Who am I to break tradition?" she said with a shrug.

Hancock unhinged himself from Sawyer's side and wrapped Chelsea in a big bear hug. "Thanks, Mom," he said.

Chelsea brushed his hair out of his eyes and laid a kiss on his forehead. And he didn't even flinch.

"Happy Birthday, Son," she said before revealing one last surprise. "I don't know about you guys, but I'm ready to ride the Poltergeist!"

All heads snapped to Chelsea.

"You're going to ride the Poltergeist?" Sawyer asked, his eyebrows nearly reaching his hairline.

"Maybe even twice," Chelsea said, fending off a serious case of collywobbles with a smug smile. "So who's going with me?"

CHAPTER 33

The café was bustling. Good thing Manny was dressed for business. His jean overall shorts and Converse high-tops provided him a boost of casual comfort, which came in handy now that the weather was warming and the café had expanded into the sunroom. More customers plus more rooms equaled more steps in a day.

After the midday rush he collapsed into a chair and reflected on how much he missed his wings, or at least what humans called wings. He chuckled at the thought of how humans pictured angels. Tall women in silky white choir robes. Gladiators with bird wings. Or, his personal favorite, fat naked babies with even tinier bird wings. It's no wonder his fellow angels had to wear these human disguises. Without his Manny disguise, the patrons of Higher Grounds Café would be screaming in terror. Chelsea wouldn't like that.

Especially not with one of her favorite customers. Marcus was back at the café for the second time that week, and Chelsea had given Manny strict instructions to spoil the kid as much as possible without his catching on. Today this included two hot chocolates and a bag of almond croissants.

"Hope you stop by again soon!" Manny walked Marcus to the door, partly out of hospitality, but also to get another glimpse of the curious scene unfolding beneath the large bay window at the café's entrance.

Soft afternoon light haloed Katrina and her Uncle Frank and bounced off the stainless steel surfaces of Frank's wheelchair. Between Frank's signature fedora and his niece's checkerboard dress, the trendy pair looked rather at odds with their quaint surroundings. But they had made themselves at home in the nook, where they had been perusing the God Blog for hours.

"Hey, Manny," Katrina said, sensing his presence for the umpteenth time. "You mind getting us a couple more of those scones?"

Manny heated two vanilla bean scones in a hurry, eager to reclaim his front row seat to their conversation. He found the exchange between believer and skeptic most enlightening. The casual observer would have certainly pegged Frank as the skeptic. According to Katrina, he had every reason to be.

"I was there when it happened," she had told him. "I saw the horse throw him. The moment he hit the ground I knew." Though five years had passed, the grief on Katrina's face was fresh, her emotions uncharacteristically visible. "And the worst part is," she continued, "it was my fault. If it weren't for me, he would have never been out that day."

For a brief moment, Manny had wondered if he was looking at Katrina from heaven's view. He could see guilt and pain flooding her eyes, but as soon as the question surfaced in his mind, she had blinked back a wave of emotion and her gaze was determined, distant. The window had closed. But Manny knew it would open again.

"What did I miss?" he asked, returning with the plate of scones.

"I'm doing it, Manny. I'm taking Uncle Frank's wager. Asking the God Blog a question." Katrina clicked away on her smartphone screen as she read her question aloud.

"Will you show me a sign? Please. Sincerely, Katherine Lorraine Phillips"

She put her phone down and looked at Frank. "I figure, if it really is God, I should use my proper name."

A moment later, Katherine Lorraine Phillips received her answer. She read it aloud.

"Dearest Katrina.

Ha! He used my preferred name!

What a delight to hear from you! Now I have a question for you. Would you be willing to take a step of faith? Also I would love to talk to you more often. Love, God."

"So, what's it gonna be?" asked Frank.

Katrina's eyes drifted off into space. She chewed her lip and twirled her dyed red hair.

Manny grinned. Over the centuries he had witnessed the transformation of innumerable honest, humble seekers. He remembered loaves and fishes and too many mouths to feed. The stirring of Bethesda's pool. Katrina? He sensed the winds of change beginning to blow.

Katrina stared at her uncle, and a smile stretched across her face.

"Oh no," Frank said. "No, no, no, no, no. You think of a different one."

"Why?"

"Because!" Frank shouted. "I stopped making this request three years ago. And believe me, I asked with all the faith I could muster. I know I'll walk again. In heaven."

"Don't make this about you, Uncle Frank. This is my prayer. My step of faith." Katrina looked to Manny, who had become the resident God Blog expert. "Tell us what to do."

Manny pulled up a chair and sat across from his coworker. He spoke with a confident tone. "Ask," he told her. "Ask with faith, faith that God will hear you and faith that God will do what is best."

"What is best? Wouldn't it be best for Uncle Frank to walk again?"

"It certainly seems so, Katrina. But prayer isn't asking God to do what we want. Prayer is asking God to do what is right."

Katrina looked back at Manny with a confused expression.

Manny glanced over at Frank. He was smiling.

"Frank," Manny said, "you get this, don't you?"

"I do, Manny." He smiled. "I've come to peace with my lot in life. God hasn't healed my body, but he has done a good work on my heart." Frank paused and looked at his niece. "Still, I am open to miracles."

Katrina's face brightened. "So am I, Uncle Frank."

Katrina glanced at Manny. He nodded. She took a deep breath and knelt beside her uncle. "I want you to ask with me too, okay?"

Frank's eyes welled with tears.

Manny leaned in.

"I think I remember how this works," Katrina said. "Now take off your hat, bow your head, and close your eyes." Katrina gripped her uncle's hands and squeezed like she was hanging on for dear life. "Dear God . . ."

Manny's eyes were wide with wonder. Rarely had he seen such an honest, selfless display of faith. Could this be the reason Katrina was drawn to the café? Manny clenched his fists, adding his own faith and hope to Katrina's prayers.

"I ask you to heal my Uncle Frank. I want to see him walk again. Please."

Katrina looked up. Frank's chin was quivering with emotion.

"I took my step of faith. Now you take yours."

Frank looked at Manny, then back at

Katrina. "Okay, I'll do it." Frank clenched his jaw and summoned his courage. He squeezed the arms of his wheelchair and began to push himself upward. As Katrina assisted Frank out of his chair, Marcus and a few onlookers gathered to witness the curious scene.

Katrina took one arm, Manny took the other. When Frank was standing, his legs began to wobble.

"Son," he said to Marcus, "pull my chair back."

Marcus hurried over and took the chair.

With the chair gone, Frank raised himself even straighter. "I'm ready." Manny and Katrina released their grips. Frank stepped, and began to fall. They grabbed him.

"It's okay," he said, once stabilized. "It's just been a while. Let me try again."

Manny looked around the café. The handful of patrons were silent. Their faces were hopeful. No sound at all, then a rush of air, a flash of light. Out of the corner of his eye he saw something, or someone, on the porch. Manny looked out the open front door.

But he didn't look long.

"I'm ready," Frank announced. This time he all but yanked himself free from their grip. He took a step, then another, then another. Straight across the room. After six steps he leaned against a table and looked back at Katrina. His face was awash with tears.

So was hers.

"God heard our prayer, Uncle Frank," she smiled.

He smiled in return. "He always has, Katrina. He always has."

CHAPTER 34

Chelsea lasted for three of Sawyer and Hancock's thirteen trips on the Poltergeist. If someone had told her a month ago that she and Sawyer would be riding roller coasters together at an amusement park, she would have been anything but amused. A month ago she could not stand the thought of Sawyer. Today his presence wasn't even bothering her. And *that* bothered her.

Chelsea was relieved to have Sara and Tony around as a buffer. "They say it's the simple things in life that make you happy. But happiness is anything but simple. Just look at us," Chelsea said to Sara as they watched Sawyer and Tony help Hancock and Emily launch rubber frogs onto metal lily pads in hopes of winning a giant unicorn. Hancock had already claimed an oversized octopus with tentacles that had just begun to glow in the dark.

Hancock and Emily were never as happy

as when their dad was around, and nothing made Chelsea happier than seeing her children thrive. As much as she tried to distance herself from Sawyer, her happiness would always be tied to him.

"Sawyer seems to be doing really well these days," Sara said. "You know he told Tony he's been talking to one of his pastor friends in Austin?"

"Good for him," Chelsea said. "I want him to be better, ya know? For the kids."

"Score!" Sawyer's cheer carried over to the breezy cabana where Chelsea and Sara were waiting. Hancock's frog had landed smack-dab on the middle of a lily pad.

"We won, Mom!" Emily waved her trophy like a true champion.

"Impressive!" Chelsea called as the group came to join them.

"Mom, can we stay for the fireworks? Dad said we need to ask you," Emily said.

"Well, Uncle Tony and Aunt Sara probably have to get home to the babysitter. Plus they have church tomorrow."

"Well, maybe Dad could take us home?" Hancock asked.

"Well . . ." Chelsea scanned the group for reactions. Everyone was nodding.

Thanks for the moral support, Sara.

"Okay . . . if you're sure that's okay?" she

asked Sawyer.

"I'd be happy to be your chauffeur," he said, dipping his head in a bow.

Emily curtsied. *"Gracias, señor."*

"I guess that's settled then," Chelsea said. But she wasn't feeling so settled inside. This was the first time they had been together, just the four of them, since the separation. She didn't want the kids to get the wrong idea. Or Sawyer either, for that matter.

Their last exchange drifted through her head more than once as the evening progressed.

I have every reason I need to divorce you.

I know you do, but I'm going to keep hoping you don't.

Would he feel the same way after she delivered the divorce papers? Chelsea knew she could do life alone. She had proven it to herself and to everyone else. But did she want to?

She banished the thought as soon as it entered her mind, blaming the elaborate fireworks and lack of adult company. She didn't have to worry about that anymore. After all, she had options. Dennis Darling told her she had an open road. Full of possibilities!

"There are a lot of really great opportunities right now," Sawyer said as they cruised down the highway, kids snoozing in the backseat. "In both Austin and San Antonio."

Chelsea had not seen Sawyer this enthused in a long time. At least not over anything so unremarkable. It was strange how the tables had turned. Here Sawyer was in the middle of a job hunt, while she was running a successful business. A million-dollar business.

"I always knew I wanted to get into coaching," he continued. "I just wasn't ready to humble myself and do it. But this might be the hard reset I need for my life. Plus I can be nearby, you know? As close as you want me to be."

"That sounds wonderful," Chelsea said.

Wait, what am I saying? Close isn't wonderful.

Sawyer's magnetic field was scrambling the data, so neatly stored and sorted in her brain. "Austin would be a great fit," she said.

And a forty-minute drive at least.

Sawyer's face fell a bit. "Yeah, we'll see . . ." he said.

They rode the rest of the way in silence.

Chelsea forced her reeling mind to the café and the mouth-watering, multilayer cake waiting for her in the kitchen. She hadn't heard from Manny and Katrina since morning, so she assumed the day had been uneventful.

But the moment Sawyer pulled into the drive, Chelsea knew something was wrong. The front door of the café was swinging on its hinges in the wind. Shattered glass covered the porch. A trail of shards led to the supply closet, where coffee beans had spilled onto the floor in a heaping pile. But these were the least of Chelsea's worries.

The router was missing. The God Blog was gone.

CHAPTER 35

"Take the kids and get back in the car. I'll call the police." Sawyer handed his keys to Chelsea.

"C'mon, kids." Chelsea scooped up little Emily and raced out the door with Hancock beside her.

"Who would do this, Mom?" Hancock asked as they piled into Sawyer's black Escalade.

"I don't know, honey."

"What's Daddy doing?"

"He's making sure you're safe."

For the first time in a very long time — so long she couldn't remember when — Chelsea was relieved that Sawyer was with them. From behind tinted glass she watched as one by one the windows of her café and living quarters were illuminated as Sawyer launched his own investigation. When the police arrived, they confirmed his findings: only the router was stolen, and there seemed

206

to be no immediate danger.

By the time the police had filed their report and left the scene, it was well past midnight. Chelsea's original plan was to find a hotel for herself and the kids, but Emily was now fast asleep in the backseat, and Chelsea hated the idea of waking her.

"Can't we just stay here? Dad could stay too," Hancock suggested.

Sawyer looked to Chelsea. "I could sleep on the couch downstairs. You'd have to be crazy to mess with an NFL all-star, right?"

"Yeah, sure. That's probably a good idea."

As Sawyer lifted the sleeping Emily from his SUV, he couldn't keep the grin off his face. Chelsea hoped this wasn't a mistake.

After a restless night, Chelsea overslept, then descended the stairs to find an eerie, unsettling scene playing out in the café: her world, running without her. Manny and Katrina were reorganizing the raided pantry. Hancock and Emily were quietly eating breakfast at a table. Sawyer and Bo were replacing the broken glass. Chelsea toured the scene like a ghost, invisible and unnoticed.

"Well, good morning, everyone!" she declared.

"Hey, Chels!" Sawyer glanced up from his

window repair, looking way too at home in her home.

Manny and Katrina raced over to her. "Thank God you and the kids weren't here when this happened," Manny said.

"Yeah, I'm grateful," Chelsea said. "But I'm still worried. What do you think our customers will say when they discover the God Blog is gone?"

When the café opened, Chelsea got her answer, and it was much worse than she imagined. With Sawyer Chambers in the house, the café had a new star. Of course there were disgruntled and disappointed customers, but Sawyer had a way with people like no other. He could turn snark into a smile in a matter of seconds. By lunchtime he was drawing his own crowd, signing autographs, taking photos with football fans, and charming even the athletically illiterate. When he rounded the corner with a giant slab of her precious multilayer cake, Chelsea had seen enough. There was no way Sawyer Chambers was going to have her cake and eat it too.

She marched upstairs to her bedroom and grabbed the legal envelope stowed in her dresser.

Petition for Dissolution of Marriage. The words no longer appeared stiff and formal;

they leapt off the page, calling for Chelsea to join the ranks of the dreaded 50 percent. She signed her name on the dotted line and headed downstairs. It was time to let Sawyer know he had been drafted.

At the first opportunity to speak with him alone, she handed him the packet.

"You already signed it?" Sawyer's jaw clenched as he steadied himself on the stainless steel kitchen counter.

Chelsea wasn't sure if he was holding back a tirade or tears.

"Delaying the process will only confuse the kids," she said, holding her ground. "Having you stay the night and hang out in the café probably isn't helping either. Not that I don't appreciate your assistance."

"Here," Sawyer said after an unsettling stretch of silence. He extended the papers to Chelsea.

"What?"

"I can't sign these."

"What do you mean you can't sign? You already agreed to this!" Chelsea's voice rose and dipped as she spoke.

"Well, I don't agree anymore," he said, slamming the envelope on the counter.

"Don't make this harder than it has to be. I'll just send them to your lawyer."

"Do what you have to do."

"Chelsea?" Manny swung through the doorway, but the tension in the room stopped him in his tracks. "Sorry."

"No problem," Sawyer grumbled. "I was just leaving."

Manny escaped into the café as Sawyer stomped toward the door.

"Don't leave like that, Sawyer," Chelsea called.

Sawyer stopped, turning on his heel. His intensity radiated through the room. "What do you want me to do, Chelsea? If you tell me to stay, I will stay. I can't promise to be perfect. But I hope to be the kind of man you want to have around. The kind of man you want to raise a family with and share a home with. I am becoming that man. I'm doing it for Hancock and Emily and for myself. And I'm doing it for you. Because I love you, and I'm in love with you. So just tell me what you want me to do, and I'll do it."

Chelsea sank onto the stool behind her. The wind had been knocked from her chest.

"I think you should go," she said in a small voice. She hoped she wouldn't come to regret it.

CHAPTER 36

"Mr. Darling will see you now."

Chelsea followed a curvy brunette through Dennis Darling's swanky office in the Alamo Heights district. The rhythmic tapping of the young woman's six-inch heels might as well have been a wagging finger, ridiculing Chelsea for her wardrobe choice. Chelsea had hoped her linen ensemble and matching flats would exude an air of casual confidence, but in this ultramodern office she felt as out of place as Betty Crocker. The homemade layer cake in her hands didn't help.

"And what can I do for you today, Chelsea?" asked the George Clooney of San Antonio real estate.

"I hope you like raspberry chocolate layer cake!" Chelsea entered Mr. Darling's office, presenting her decadent creation.

"Thank you." But that darling grin was missing.

"I was hoping we could resume our conversation. You know, from last week," Chelsea said.

"Britney, we'll just be a moment," Dennis said to his office assistant, who promptly closed the door and clicked her way back to her workstation.

Dennis turned his chair to face Chelsea. "And how is the Higher Grounds Café? Now that the God Blog is gone."

"Well . . ." That was the question of the hour.

There was no denying that, after six solid days without her café's famous blog, business had declined. In her first three months Chelsea had managed to make her monthly $9,555.64 tax payment without too much difficulty. But with added business came added expenses: the new ovens, the parlor remodel, her two employees, not to mention the cost of providing for her and the children. Chelsea had managed to make her April payment with just a few hundred dollars to spare. With five more payments to go, Chelsea was grateful Hancock and Emily didn't mind peanut butter and jelly sandwiches. Still, she was ready to relieve herself of the burden.

"Business is okay," Chelsea continued. "I want you to know I've been thinking about our conversation. A lot, actually. I have a scenario that I think might interest you."

"Oh?"

"Partners. I could sell you 50 percent ownership of the café for half the number we discussed. Of course I'd still be managing the day-to-day affairs."

"And what was that number exactly?"

Chelsea folded and unfolded her hands. Why was he making this so difficult? Where was that trademark charm?

"Well . . ." Chelsea's mouth felt dry, nearly too dry to speak. "One million dollars is the figure we discussed. But I'm proposing half."

"So five hundred thousand?"

"Yes."

"For 50 percent ownership?"

"Exactly."

"And all this without that magic little blog of yours?"

Chelsea shifted in her chair. "Yeah . . . The blog was never really under my control. Per se."

"Hmm. So this" — Dennis pulled his cell phone from his sport coat pocket — "was not your doing? Per se?" Dennis showed Chelsea a text message he had received. It was a picture of an entry from the God Blog:

213

"I know all your secrets, even the one tucked inside your wallet. If you only knew the gift I have for you and who you are speaking to, you would ask me, and I would give you living water. I would cleanse you from the inside out. I love you. I always have, and I always will. God."

Chelsea remembered the entry. "Um . . . nope. Definitely not me. Like I said, I really didn't have anything to do with the answers on that blog."

"So it was God?" Dennis's tone was unpleasant, uncharming, and altogether undarling.

"I really can't say if —"

"You want me to believe that the woman I was seeing — who just happens to be a personal friend of yours — asked a question at a blog in *your* café and got a very personal answer from some all-knowing God? Why would he — or should I say she — break up a relationship between two consenting adults? Jealousy perhaps?"

"I'm sorry, I really had no idea —"

"About the hotel key in Deb's wallet?"

"What? No!" Chelsea waved her hands as if to deflect Dennis's accusatory bullets. But then an idea struck, one that made too much sense to ignore. Chelsea stood and pointed an accusing finger at Dennis. "You! I told you where I kept the router. How do I know you didn't steal it from my café? After all, your other business, Café Cosmos, is certainly benefitting from my misfortune!"

"Do you realize how crazy you sound? You know what? Forget it. I'm not interested in you or your café. Or 50 percent ownership. Or whatever blogging scheme you come up with to market your next business venture." Dennis swiveled in his chair to face his laptop. "Oh, and I'm allergic to raspberries."

Chelsea exited Dennis Darling's office, cake in hand, her mind racing as she put the puzzle pieces together. Deb Kingsly, the quintessential Alamo Heights housewife, and . . . Dennis Darling? To think that Chelsea had been flattered by that cheating, thieving grin. At least whoever, or whatever, was on the other side of that blog had steered Deb in the right direction.

Chelsea held back a wave of emotion as she fumbled for her keys, all the while balancing her perfectly delicious raspberry chocolate cake. Once again she was left with a painful realization. There would be no partnerships. No 50 percents. No tax relief. No fairy godmother to whisk her away in a magic pumpkin. Chelsea was on her own.

Though she did manage to find one silver lining. In her rearview mirror, of all places. As Chelsea drove away, she relished one last glance at her delectable raspberry chocolate cake splattered across the windshield of Mr. Darling's shiny BMW.

Chapter 37

The courtyard of the convent for the Sisters of Divine Providence had become of place of refuge for Manny, particularly during Evensong. There was something familiar about the angelic choir, their sacred songs wafting through the night in perfect harmony; he always felt close to heaven here. And heaven knows he was missing his holy home. He had not seen or heard from Gabriel in weeks. The lack of communication was taking its toll on Manny. And on the Higher Grounds Café, no doubt.

The soft grass welcomed him as he sank to his knees, inviting the worship to wash away the cares of the day. But his mind raced against the tempo of the choral melody, his clamoring thoughts creating a dissonance only Manny could hear. He felt like the conductor of an orchestra gone rogue.

Rest! Manny forced his mind into a moment of stillness before allowing his thoughts to resume at a more melodic rhythm.

How had he allowed the God Blog to be stolen? Why hadn't he been warned? Had he failed Chelsea and, even worse, God? Was this apparent silence from the heavens his punishment?

Staccato beads of sweat dripped off his anxious forehead. His heart was beating like a bass line. He had never felt so human, so weak. He knew the ultimate victory belonged to heaven, but that did not mean every battle would be won.

The spirit is willing, but the body is weak.

The words came through loud and clear, a calming refrain written by the Maestro himself. Manny recalled the great oratorio, first heard in a garden called Gethsemane. He found comfort in knowing he was not alone in his distress. Heaven had not abandoned him. Nor would heaven abandon Manny.

Not my will, but your will be done.

The words struck a chord with Manny as never before. He repeated them aloud with resolve. "Not my will, but your will be done."

Chapter 38

Chelsea winced at the price tag inside the shiny new sneakers Hancock had picked. "How 'bout we look at a different store, bud?"

"Fine." Hancock shrugged.

Chelsea led her sulking son through Rivercenter Mall's grand atrium where a mariachi band played an upbeat, festive tune. Chelsea had imagined a mother-son shoe-shopping spree would be a welcome distraction from the stresses of the café and their changing family dynamic. Instead, it was a painful reminder of their new walk of life. The last time she had taken Hancock shopping, they left the mall with boxes of new shoes, and she hadn't even looked at the price tags. Today she could hardly afford to replace the Air Jordans bursting at the seams on Hancock's feet.

Chelsea could recall similar moments from her own teenaged years, shopping with her mom for off-brand Dr. Martens. At school the next day she had felt just as inferior as the imitation leather boots on her feet. She survived, and so would Hancock. That's what she had been telling herself the last few days, as she worked up enough courage to broach the long overdue divorce conversation with her son.

"So, Hancock." Chelsea tiptoed into the topic. "I've been wanting to talk to you about —"

"Yeah, I know. And I don't really want to talk about it right now, Mom."

"Okay . . ."

"But when it happens, I wanna live with Dad." Hancock bolted past Chelsea, avoiding the inevitable pain his admission would bring to his mom.

Chelsea paused to give her son some space — and herself a moment to breathe. She had to hold it together. At least until she made it home. She had accepted that her family needed a new rule book. It had just never occurred to her that she wouldn't be the only one writing the rules.

Chelsea caught up with Hancock, her emotions in full control. "What about these?" she said, pointing to a pair of monochromatic slip-on Vans.

"Hmm . . . They're okay," he said, attempting politeness. "I like these more though."

Chelsea's eyebrows rose at the sight of her son's choice of footwear: skater lace-ups emblazoned with fluorescent graffiti. At least the price was right. "Great. Let's get 'em."

Hancock stole a glance at the price tag. "Can we still go out for dinner?"

"We'll grab a burger and a milkshake before we leave."

"Really?"

Graffiti sneakers and junk food. Chelsea was already abiding by the newest rule in her rule book: Choose battles. Carefully.

CHAPTER 39

Chelsea slid into the last pew beside Hancock and Emily midway through a standing ovation, for what she didn't catch. Without the draw of the God Blog, she had to make the most of every opportunity to earn extra cash. On Sundays that meant arriving at the church an hour early and entertaining chatty church members until they retreated into the sanctuary, sometimes well into the first half of Tony's sermon.

"What'd I miss?" Chelsea whispered to Hancock.

"There she is." A familiar voice boomed through the sanctuary, even without the aid of a microphone. "Thanks to that woman right there, and the work God has done in her café and in my niece, I walked to church today. She's a saint in my book."

The congregation erupted into another round of applause. Except for Chelsea, who sat dumbfounded. She'd heard, of course, that Katrina's wheelchair-bound Uncle Frank had started to walk in her café, but she'd counted the rumor among other tall tales surrounding the God Blog. From the reuniting of long lost siblings to the discovery of grand inheritances, talk of many so-called miracles was common in the café. But she was seeing this miracle with her own eyes.

She watched in awe as Frank stepped down from the platform with ease and walked through the center aisle, right past Katrina.

I've never seen her here before.

"Chelsea Chambers, God gave you a great gift." Frank was now standing right beside Chelsea. She sank into her seat under the unwanted attention.

"With the God Blog, your café became a place for people to meet God just as they are. In the world they live in. I think we could do a better job of that here in this church," Frank said sincerely, to more applause. Chelsea's eyes darted over to Tony, who seemed to be the only one not clapping.

"As many of you know," Frank continued, "the God Blog was stolen. It was all over the news when it happened, but a week has passed and still no response. So I'd like to offer a two-thousand-dollar reward for the missing router, and I'm going to ask you all to chip in and make that number even higher. If that's okay with you, Chelsea? And Pastor, of course."

Congregants rose to their feet. Chelsea was overwhelmed by the gesture and collective support. Frank gave her a warm smile before addressing the crowd one last time. "Just meet me at the lobby café after the service. Together we can wake up our community. From the inside out!"

Frank's speech was a caffeine jolt to the congregation. A quadruple-shot buzz was coursing through the line, which now snaked around the lobby. It seemed every single member of Faith Community Church was ready and waiting to contribute. And Chelsea and Katrina were ready to serve them. With the tip jar overflowing, Chelsea made a note to find Tony and Sara and thank them for putting her on the receiving end of this generosity. But they found her first.

"It isn't right, Chelsea," Tony said, pulling her aside. "We're in the middle of remodeling the youth room, and our congregation is pouring their money into what? A marketing ploy?"

Chelsea was stunned by Tony's response. She looked to Sara, who attempted the role of a mediator.

"I think what Tony means is that there's still so much that can't be explained. Even if the God Blog is recovered. We want our congregation to be good stewards."

"All of this —" Tony gestured to the line of people Katrina was serving. "It's a distraction."

"So you want me to leave?" Chelsea asked. Neither Tony nor Sara answered, which was answer enough. "I see," she said, fighting back a string of words that should never be uttered in church.

Just before Chelsea lost the fight, Sara interrupted, her face filled with concern. "Hi, Marcus. Are you okay?"

Chelsea turned to see her youngest regular customer, his shoulders sloped beneath the weight of his blue backpack, his face drenched with tears.

"Mrs. Chelsea, I'm so . . ." Marcus struggled to speak. His slim frame shook with each sob. "I'm so . . . here." The boy wiped his tears on his sleeves and pulled the backpack from his shoulder, handing it to Chelsea.

Chelsea tentatively tugged at the zipper. Nestled amongst comic books and dirty clothes was the missing router, no longer glowing but completely intact.

"Marcus . . ."

"I'm sorry, Mrs. Chelsea. I'm so sorry."

"But why?" Chelsea asked, placing her arm on the boy's shoulder. In spite of his transgression, her soft spot for Marcus remained.

"My mom. She's real sick. Like really, really sick. And I thought maybe . . ." His eyes drifted toward Frank, who was bowed in prayer with another church member. "My mom had a question for the God Blog. But it didn't even work in the hospital." The young boy's eyes filled with tears once again. "I didn't mean to ruin it for everyone."

"Come here." Chelsea pulled Marcus into an embrace. "Sometimes we do the wrong thing for the right reason. We've all been there." Chelsea glanced at Tony, who looked away. "But you're doing the right thing now, and that's what counts the most."

Marcus nodded.

"So where's your mom now?" Sara asked. "It's been a while since she's been in church. We've missed her."

"Santa Rosa Hospital. I'm taking the bus there now."

"You can ride with me. I'm coming with

you," Chelsea said, much to everyone's surprise.

"What?" Marcus asked.

"I still haven't asked the God Blog a question. She can have mine."

The boy's face brightened one hundred watts, which only darkened the grim expressions Sara and Tony wore. Marcus scampered across the lobby toward the door.

"Manny, will you take the router back to the café?" Chelsea said.

"This is ridiculous!" Tony spoke through gritted teeth.

"I'll just ask the question for her."

"Chelsea . . ." Sara interjected.

"What?" Chelsea said sharply. "We have to do what we can to help this family."

CHAPTER 40

"Is it working yet?" Chelsea waited as Manny tinkered with the router on the other end of the line. "It is? Oh, thank God! Be sure to let everyone know. In fact, post a sign. I'm at the hospital now. I shouldn't be too long."

She followed Marcus around the corridor to a row of sterile hospital elevators — where she found Tony and Sara waiting for them. They had accepted Chelsea's challenge and were ready to do what they could to help Marcus and his family.

"The God Blog is up," Chelsea said, keeping her tone and emotions at bay. She could almost see Tony biting his tongue.

"My mom's on the tenth floor," Marcus said.

Tenth floor. ICU. Chelsea had scanned the sign at the hospital entry.

The elevator ride was long and silent. Marcus left Tony, Sara, and Chelsea in the hall so he could prepare his mom for visitors.

"I still think this is a bad idea," Tony said. "As a pastor I can tell you this: pat answers don't fly in hospitals."

Before Chelsea could respond, Marcus returned. "You can come in, but she's not doing too good today," he said.

They followed Marcus into the room where Desiree Johnson lay, her skeletal frame wracked by cancer. Burrowed deep beneath her brows were honey-colored eyes that no longer sparkled but managed to glimmer at the sight of her son. Chelsea gripped her sister's hand, steeling herself at the heartbreaking sight.

"Mama, this is Chelsea, the lady with that website."

"Hi, Desiree," Chelsea said. "I heard you have a question you wanted to ask the God Blog." She flinched at her own words. They sounded trite in such desperate circumstances.

Desiree gave a grateful nod, then turned to her son. "Will you step outside, baby?"

Once Marcus stepped into the hall, Desiree motioned for her visitors to be seated on a bench beneath the lone window in her stark room.

"Thank you all for coming, especially you,

Pastor," Desiree said.

Tony stroked his chin, concealing a quiver. "Desiree . . . we had no idea," he said, looking to Sara, who had tears forming in her eyes. "I'm so sorry."

"You don't have to apologize. I'm glad for the chance to see you again. And to meet you," she said, fixing her gaze on Chelsea. "You've been good to Marcus. Thank you."

Chelsea forced a weak smile.

"I only have one question for God before I go. Everything else can be answered in heaven."

"And what's that?" Chelsea's voice trembled.

A gentle stream of tears began to trickle down Desiree's face. "Besides my precious boy, the only family I have is my mom. She doesn't have long on this earth, so I want to know . . . Who will take care of Marcus when I'm gone?"

Chelsea took the long way home. The trials and tribulations of her own family had cordoned her off from the world around her. But the harrowing sight of Marcus gripping his dying mother's hand had pierced through the isolating veil. The extra scones and hot chocolates she'd been giving the child seemed trivial in the light of his

230

overwhelming need. The desperation in Desiree's eyes, the pure-hearted hope in Marcus's — it all made her feel so helpless. Desiree's question was forever etched in her mind. *Who will take care of Marcus when I'm gone?*

Chelsea wanted to hold her own children, to say she loved them over and over. And for a moment, albeit a passing one, Chelsea considered calling Sawyer. But alone with her thoughts, she drove on. Chelsea's SUV weaved through the sullied streets in Lavaca where Marcus lived. She proceeded through her own district of King William and wound her way through the upscale shops in Alamo Heights. She hoped to continue her journey for yet a little while more, until she spotted a rather alarming scene playing out on the crowded patio of Café Cosmos.

Sawyer. Sitting across from a redheaded beauty. He was wearing that snug blue oxford shirt he knew he looked good in. And the woman, well, she looked good and probably knew it too.

Chelsea slammed on the brakes and watched. She considered her options. She could call Sawyer on his cell, confront him on the spot. She could roll down the window and start yelling. Maybe snap a picture, find a way to use it to her advantage in the divorce proceedings.

Honk! Honk! Chelsea's scheming was interrupted by a line of cars behind her. She continued on, until she had settled on the simplest and most civilized option. She fished her cell phone from her purse, and at the next stoplight she sent Sawyer a simple text. DIVORCE PAPERS WILL ARRIVE TOMORROW.

By the time Chelsea arrived at the café, her cell phone vibrated with Sawyer's response. STILL NOT SIGNING. STILL COMMITTED TO MAKING THIS WORK WITH YOU.

Chelsea gritted her teeth. What Sawyer Chambers didn't know about commitment could fill a volume of books. Chelsea should know — she was a walking encyclopedia.

CHAPTER 41

"Excuse me, ma'am. Yes, you. Do you work here?"

Chelsea could not believe her eyes. The ginger witch who had placed her spell on Sawyer at Café Cosmos the day before was now sitting in the Higher Grounds Café. And she was calling her *ma'am*.

"It's *miss*. And I don't just work here. I am the owner of this café."

"Great," the woman said, sliding her mug toward Chelsea. "Two complaints. One, I ordered the house brew, and it's very weak. Two, your Internet is broken."

Chelsea plastered on a fake smile. "One, you're welcome to order another beverage. Two, it's not broken. In fact, it's our number one attraction." She turned to walk away.

"*Miss?* I'd like a skinny hazelnut latte. Venti, or whatever you call the biggest size here. And please make sure it's skinny."

"One large skinny hazelnut latte. Extra skinny."

"And make it to go!"

"Can I get a name?"

"Ginger."

Of course.

"I'll get that right to you, Ginger," Chelsea said with a smirk.

"You want me to get that started?" Katrina asked.

"I've got this one," Chelsea said, reaching for the heavy whipping cream.

As Chelsea brewed Ginger's latte, the pressure inside her head began to build. Sawyer had always had a weakness for gingers. Especially tall, curvy ones with a penchant for sass. Now Chelsea was steaming. She added an extra pump of sugary syrup to the latte and served it to the vixen with malicious glee. After all, revenge is sweet. At least it's supposed to be.

"It's good," Ginger said, taking a sip.

Watching Ginger consume the extra calories did not bring Chelsea near the satisfaction she'd imagined. She felt her temperature rising, her sense of propriety evaporating. She was reaching her boiling point.

Walk away, Chelsea. Quick.

"Can I get a lid for this?" Ginger piped.

234

Ginger never got her lid, but Chelsea flipped hers. In an instant her resolve vanished, and she decided she would much rather live with a tinge of guilt than a load of regret. She whirled back around.

"Look, lady. I don't know what you're trying to do here. Prove a point? I don't care. I'm done with Sawyer Chambers. He's all yours now. All the lying, drinking, cheating. The late nights and lost jobs and empty promises. And that's just the last three years! I've got decades of material. Volumes!"

"Clearly there's been some mistake." Ginger began packing up her belongings, indignant. "I am a happily married woman. It's very, very apparent you are not, but I suggest you take that up with Sawyer."

"Then what were you —"

"Ask your husband."

Ginger huffed out of the café, leaving Chelsea buried beneath a load of guilt and a mountain of regret.

It was late when Chelsea got the call from Sara. Desiree Johnson had passed away early that morning. Chelsea took the news harder than she expected. Partly because she still hadn't brought herself to ask the question of the God Blog. Now it was too

235

late. Too late for Desiree. But her question haunted Chelsea. Who would take care of Marcus?

She was on the porch worrying about the boy when a black SUV came screeching into the drive. *Sawyer.* He hopped out of the car and stormed toward her.

"That woman was interviewing me for a job, Chelsea!" Sawyer was livid.

"How was I supposed to know?"

"And she was about to hire me, but she's not anymore! I just got the call. They've retracted the offer, thanks to the stunt you pulled."

"Look, Sawyer, I'm sorry. But I see you yesterday with some hussy in tight jeans. And you're looking all cozy with your . . . your . . ." Chelsea scrambled for a defense. "Your charming face. What am I supposed to think? With your history? Potential employer is not the first thing that comes to mind! It's not even the last thing that comes to mind. And then she shows up in my café? So yeah, I got mad. Of course I got mad!"

Sawyer stared at Chelsea, shaking his head in disbelief. "Can we *not* make this about you for a moment? Every day since you left, I have taken steps in the right direction. Hard steps. All because I made you a promise that I would change. A promise I have kept because I think we have a future. A good one. But there is no way we can move forward together if you're going to hold me hostage to the past."

"But it happened! What you did. It's in the books. Forever. That's not my fault. And I'm not even saying it's your fault. It just is." Chelsea finished more calmly than she had started. When she finished speaking she was cool. Cold.

"You're never going to forgive me, are you?" Sawyer took a step back, realization setting in for the first time.

Chelsea felt her lips press together. "I don't think I know how."

CHAPTER 42

It was a rare if not unprecedented sight for Faith Community Church. Every pew was filled. And then some. Folding metal chairs lined the perimeter, and what little floor space remained was packed with standing people. From their seats in the back corner, Chelsea and the kids witnessed the Home-going Celebration of Desiree Faith Johnson.

During the rousing chorus of Desiree's favorite hymn, Chelsea couldn't take her eyes off Marcus. The young boy stood by Katrina's Uncle Frank, who had generously used the reward money he had set aside for the router to pay for the funeral expenses. Through tears the boy lifted his voice. "I sing because I'm happy! I sing because I'm free! His eye is on the sparrow, and I know He watches me!"

Through the life of Marcus's mother, the Lord had indeed watched over the sparrows of the Lavaca neighborhood. From the stories of loved ones, Chelsea pieced together a portrait of a rare and generous soul.

"No one would take me in. But then I met Desiree . . ."

"I hadn't eaten in three days, and then Desiree . . ."

"My husband was in prison. We had nowhere to go, not a prayer left to pray, but then . . ."

There it was again: Desiree, the turning point in each story. The loving embrace, the healing word, the generous gift. Desiree's humble apartment was a crossroads for the needy and downcast.

Chelsea could learn from her example. And from the looks of it, she wasn't the only one.

Tony stood behind the pulpit to offer the closing benediction. "Blessed are the poor in spirit, for theirs is the kingdom of heaven. Blessed are those who mourn . . ." Tony glanced up from his pages of prepared notes. His eyes welled with tears as they met the gaze of so many mourners. At long last, his church was full, overflowing even. Though Chelsea guessed this was hardly the crowd he had imagined filling his pews.

Tony looked down at his notes and began again. "Blessed are those who mourn . . ." But once again he could not finish. Something was amiss. Gone were Tony's comforting smile and practiced pastoral demeanor. Though he hardly knew Desiree Faith Johnson, Pastor Tony was undone with emotion. His head fell to the podium, and the sanctuary echoed with his sobs.

Sara approached Tony, placed her arm on his shoulder, and picked up where he had left off. "Blessed are those who mourn, for they shall be comforted."

Chelsea startled at the sound of someone pounding against the front door of her café. It was ten p.m., far too late for customers. She hurried down the stairs, her phone ready in case of emergency. When she flipped on the lights she saw Tony standing under a torrent of rain.

"Tony! What are you doing out there?" Chelsea rushed to unlock the door.

Tony entered, disheveled and soaking wet, though far more composed than when Chelsea had seen him at the funeral just hours before. "I'm sorry. I would have called, but I lost my phone sometime today. I wasn't thinking when I left the house."

"Are Sara and the kids all right?"

"They're fine. I'm here for me, actually. I was hoping I could look at the God Blog. For myself this time."

"Yes, of course. Anything you need. Coffee?"

"That'd be nice."

Tony settled in at a tea table near the register while Chelsea prepared them both a mug of caffeinated comfort.

"Listen to this one," Tony said, perusing his laptop screen. Chelsea sat across from her brother-in-law with their coffees and a few scones.

"Dear God (if this really is you), I hate the church. I hate religion and everything about it. It seems so obvious that religion causes more problems than it solves. It manipulates and separates people with fear. The church is nothing more than a place for people to pose as someone they're not. How can you defend all this hypocrisy?"

Chelsea chuckled. "That's from someone named Spencer, if I remember correctly."

"You're good," Tony said.

"Dear Spencer, I don't even try to defend hypocrisy. Now I have a question for you. Do you really think I started that? Don't you think I've had my fill of worship charades, religious games, and fearmongering, as you and your friends say? You think I want this? No thank you.

Yet, Spencer, I haven't seen much compassion out of you, have I? You pride yourself in authenticity, yet behave like everyone in your own circle. You make irreligion a religion. Leave the hypocrites up to me. And from time to time, look up. Focus on me. I think you might be surprised by what you'll find. Love, God."

"Not a bad answer, huh?" Chelsea said.

"Not bad," Tony said.

Chelsea left Tony to himself while she deep-cleaned the curved glass of her pastry display case. After more than an hour of reading from the blog, Chelsea noticed Tony wiping his teary eyes on the sleeve of his already damp sweatshirt. She brought a few napkins to the table.

"So you still think I'm writing these pat answers?" Chelsea asked.

"No, of course not. I guess it could be God. Or maybe it isn't." Tony closed his laptop. He looked up at Chelsea, his eyes red and puffy. "What gets me the most is the questions — all the hopes, fears, and doubts. The needs! From people right here in my own backyard. And I've been raising money for new carpeting." He stopped to dry his eyes once more. "Something tells me Desiree Johnson paid very little mind to paint colors and multimedia youth rooms."

"She passed away before I could post her question to the God Blog."

" 'Who will take care of Marcus when I'm gone?' " Tony recalled. "I'm glad you didn't ask."

"Why's that?"

"Because I hope to be the answer."

CHAPTER 43

"Dennis said he spoke to you."

"Um . . . yes." Chelsea had planned to deposit Deb's latte on the table, exchange niceties, and dash. But it was clear Deb had come to talk, so Chelsea took a seat across from her old friend, proceeding gingerly. "So you guys are still —"

"No. I ended it," Deb said. "He still calls and leaves me messages. I used to listen to them, but I promised my husband I wouldn't do that anymore. I actually have a new number now. I'll give it to you. I hope this doesn't make you uncomfortable," she added matter-of-factly. "It's just that after months of sneaking around, honesty is cathartic."

Chelsea nodded. "And your husband . . . How are you guys handling everything?"

"I knew I married a good man. I didn't realize how good." Deb reached for the napkin beneath her mug of coffee and dabbed her eyes. "Of course, it hasn't been easy on him. He's heartbroken. It's a process, a painful one. But sometimes I think he's more forgiving of me than I am of myself."

Chelsea moved to the seat next to Deb, placing her arm around her old friend.

"Sorry." Deb tried to collect herself. "It's hard because I know I don't deserve it. But the way he's loved me through this. It makes me love him even more."

Deb's eyes drifted toward the window, and the two women sat in silence.

Chelsea felt for Deb. She really did. But in the back of her mind, she had to acknowledge that her friend was the Sawyer of her situation. What made Deb's deed forgivable? How did her husband manage to move past the past? Chelsea began to wonder if there was something wrong with her. She knew she had a tendency to hold grudges, but maybe there was something more. Maybe she had a genetic predisposition for holding grudges. With her family history it made sense. Broken and battered branches ran down her father's side of the family tree. It was simply in her nature. Chelsea was missing the forgiveness gene.

"Chelsea?" Deb said after some time had passed. "Isn't that your dad?"

Chelsea stood to her feet, pressing her nose against the front window like a little girl. Sure enough, her father was shuffling toward the café, wearing tweed pants, a blue oxford, and navy blue slippers. The closer he got, the more out of sorts he appeared, his voice carrying down the street.

"Virginia!" he shouted. "Virginia!" He bellowed for his late ex-wife as he made his way onto the lawn.

Chelsea knocked on the window instinctively, hoping this would make him stop, but it only seemed to amplify his efforts. She stepped outside to prevent the scene from escalating. It worked, but not in the way she anticipated.

"Virginia," he whispered with relief. He grasped onto the rail of the porch, his shoulders hunched, chest heaving. "Where are the girls? I came home and they were gone. The car's missing too."

Chelsea stared at her father. He was lost. No, more than lost. He was trapped. Trapped in time.

"Answer me, Virginia! Are the girls all right?"

"Mommy?" Emily had arrived home from school. Hancock trailed her by a couple yards.

"Chelsea!" the old man exclaimed. "I'm

so sorry, Chelsea. I never should have left you like that. Daddy loves you. You know that, right? I'll always love you." He knelt down in front of Emily, kissing her forehead. His affection for the child, though misled, was undeniable. Even to Chelsea.

Emily looked to her mom, her eyes full of questions and a hint of fear. No wonder Chelsea's father had mistaken the little girl for his own daughter.

"Come, Charlie," Chelsea said, helping her father to his feet.

"Mom, is that your dad?" Hancock asked.

Chelsea nodded. Hancock knew very little about his grandfather, but he knew it was no accident they had not yet met him. "Let's go inside," he whispered, leading Emily by the hand.

"And Sara? She's okay?" Charlie asked.

"She's just fine."

"I'm so sorry, Virginia. I hope you can forgive me," he said, closing the gap between them. Chelsea's first instinct was to step back. To go inside and shut out the man who had slammed the door on her so many years ago. But something stopped her. Pity.

A strong wind blew through the trees, tinkling through the wind chimes Katrina had added to her front porch. She and her father both looked up, watching the branches bend and sway in the steely sky.

She looked back at the shivering old man, exposed to the crowd of onlookers who had been disturbed by his confused ranting.

"Come on, Charlie," Chelsea said, placing an arm on her father's shoulder. "Let's get you inside."

CHAPTER 44

"Look at my girls! So beautiful." Charlie beamed at a photo of Chelsea and Sara dressed in frilly pastels. "That was Easter Sunday, three years ago."

Chelsea and her father sat on the sofa in the sunroom, an open photo album between them. Chelsea looked at the photo with amazement. Her father's memory was sharp as ever. Only it seemed to have stopped at 1980.

"That was a great day. One of our best," Charlie said, soaking in the memory.

Chelsea's attempt to bring clarity to her father only seemed to muddy the waters, so she resolved to make the past the present until Sara arrived. Her mother's old room was like a time capsule, filled with memories that seemed to calm her father's confused mind.

Charles reached across the sofa and took Chelsea's hand, still confusing her for his late wife. "You remember, don't you, Virginia?"

Of course she did. Chelsea remembered everything. The moment she found her mother doubled over in the kitchen weeping, stinging from the discovery of Charlie's infidelity. The neglect of her father, which led to a nearly fatal car wreck, scarring her and her sister in different ways. The years of silence broken by an invitation to a shotgun wedding. The rage that followed. The shame she felt, walking down the aisle alone. And then there was the man at the end of the aisle. Sawyer Chambers, his own failings, so reminiscent of her father's.

No wonder Chelsea's memory had become her greatest weapon, a sword she wielded, wounding others to protect herself. For decades she had waged this war, but at what cost? Now she stood alone on the battlefield, bleeding and bruised. There were no victors in this war, and Chelsea counted herself among the casualties.

Was it time to lay down the sword?

"Yes, Charles. I remember," Chelsea said, playing the role of her mother. "You bought Chelsea an Easy-Bake Oven that afternoon," she said, pointing out a photo of herself running a makeshift kitchen at the ripe old age of eight.

Charlie's grin stretched a mile wide. "Does she still play with that? 'Cause she loved that thing. And you know what? She made some delicious stuff. Like gourmet kind of stuff!"

Now it was Chelsea's turn to smile. Her chocolate mini cakes were anything but gourmet, but her father's commentary made the memory sweeter.

It was a strange phenomenon, watching the past bring healing instead of hurt. Through page after page of her mother's photo albums, Chelsea narrated a rosy picture of Christmases past, birthdays, first days of school. For once she wielded her memory not to wound, but to heal. They traveled through time, until landing on a timeless bridal portrait: Chelsea, wearing her mother's antique wedding dress. She fell silent, uncertain of what to say.

"You were the most beautiful bride," Charlie said, giving Chelsea's hand a squeeze. She returned the squeeze, then freed her hand to wipe the tears forming in her eyes.

"Thank you," she said. "That means a lot. More than you know."

He nodded, glancing at the bay window behind him, where the sun had begun to set. "Well, I better go now," he said, standing to his feet. "Deadlines and all." He felt in his pockets. "Have you seen my keys?"

"Dad?" Sara stood in the doorway, her face somewhere between surprise and concern.

Charlie looked from Sara to Chelsea. "Do you know her?"

Chelsea offered Sara a bewildered shrug.

"Where are my keys?" Charlie said, his temper flaring. "I lost my keys!"

"We'll find them," Chelsea said, patting down the sofa until she felt a cool metal edge. She pulled the keys from their hiding place. "See? They're not lost."

As Chelsea extended the key ring to her father, her eyes landed on a relic dangling amongst the keys. Two bottle caps painted red and blue. Glued inside the ridged edges of each cap was a photo, one of Sara and one of Chelsea. She had made the key chain for Father's Day when she was seven.

"Thank you," Charlie said, clutching the bottle caps in his wrinkly palm. The familiar rhythmic jingling returned as he placed the keys in his pocket. He eased onto the couch. His face relaxed.

"Is he like this most of the time?" Chelsea asked, taking in her father's distant stare.

"You never know these days."

Chelsea had entered a door into the past,

albeit an alternate past, unlocked by a man no longer imprisoned by bitter memories. For years she had felt like the forgotten daughter. Unwanted. Unloved. And yet there was her father, holding her in the palm of his hand. Still, it was bittersweet. Charles Hancock no longer possessed the key to conscious reconciliation. That door was sealed.

"There are still some ways to connect," Sara said, always looking for the bright side. "Photos are good. And he likes music."

Chelsea looked over at the phonograph in the corner. Her father had taught her to two-step while listening to a Sinatra album. Maybe this time she could teach him?

Sawyer's black Escalade rolled to a halt in front of the Higher Grounds Café. His game plan was simple: drop off the signed divorce papers and leave. No hello, no visit with the kids, no arguing about the past. There'd be plenty of time for that in the future.

"Leavin' already?"

Sawyer turned to see Chelsea's neighbor. "Hey there."

"It's Bo," the old man said, stepping into the light of the streetlamp. "We fixed the broken window together."

"Of course, Bo. Good to see you," he said,

shaking the man's hand. Sawyer's eyes darted to and fro. He was hoping to deliver the papers unnoticed.

"How's the job search? Any good leads?"

"Challenging. I had an interview for a coaching position at the community college today, so we'll see. I'm headed back to Austin now. I just had to drop something off."

"You got a special family in there." Bo gestured toward the café. "You do know that, right?"

Sawyer braved a look at the house above the café. Through the window of Hancock and Emily's bedroom he could see a constellation of stars, projected from the nightlight he had given them. "I do know that. Didn't always, but I do now."

"Well, you have a safe trip back to Austin," Bo said as he turned to leave. "Hope to see you soon."

Sawyer lingered for just a moment more, hoping to catch a glimpse of his children. But it was late, and Hancock and Emily would most likely be dreaming. As Sawyer rounded the corner of his SUV, a curious flash of light caught his eye. He glanced over his shoulder toward the newly remodeled sunroom. In his thirteen years of marriage to Chelsea, Sawyer had never witnessed a scene such as this. Chelsea was dancing.

But with whom, he could not tell. Sawyer crept forward for a better look, sticking close to the shadows of a nearby tree.

The realization hit him like a quarterback sack, hard and unexpected. Chelsea was dancing with her father, the man she had sworn she'd never forgive.

CHAPTER 45

From her mother's rocker, Chelsea watched the brewing storm. After a whirlwind week, she was grateful for a quiet afternoon in her café.

"Hey, boss." Manny trudged into the sunroom, holding a bouquet of pure white flowers.

"What are these for?" Chelsea asked.

"It's Resurrection weekend. Good Friday, actually. I thought you could use something cheery in here."

"They're lovely."

"Easter lilies. From my sisters' garden."

"Tell your sisters thank you. You should bring them by the café sometime."

Manny placed them on the center table, then handed Chelsea the day's mail. Among the colorful coupons and black-and-white bills, there was a familiar-looking manila envelope. "Thanks, Manny." Chelsea started to open the envelope, but noticed Manny was still standing beside her. "Are you okay?"

"Yeah," Manny said. His eyes were glistening and sincere. "I just hope I'm doing a good job for you is all."

"Are you kidding? It's because of you I feel like I can make it on my own." But when Manny looked to the floor, Chelsea wondered if she had said the wrong thing. "Are you okay?"

"Yes, ma'am."

Chelsea decided to lighten the mood. "I like your T-shirt, Manny," she added.

"Katrina got it for me. It's a *Star Wars* shirt."

"I see that."

Manny forced a smile before leaving Chelsea alone with the dreaded manila envelope.

As Chelsea presumed, these were indeed the documents that would end her marriage. It was over. Chelsea was free. Her life was an open road. But if she continued on this path, her only companions would be the bitter memories that would stalk her until she could remember them no more. Her father had blazed this trail.

At eighty years old, he was finally free. But what a dreadful salvation! His freedom came by no conscious choice of his own, but rather by the cruel saviors of Alzheimer's and dementia.

Chelsea knew it was too late to turn back. She was holding the evidence in her hands. Now she had to learn to walk the lonely road she had paved for herself. But how?

How will I make it on my own?

CHAPTER 46

Manny sat in an empty movie theater with his eyes glued to the sprawling screen and his hand burrowed in a giant tub of popcorn. He had come to savor this new post-work routine of evening prayer and late-night movies, and he had been looking forward to this special showing of *The Empire Strikes Back* for weeks. Hancock told him it was the best of all the *Star Wars* movies. Halfway through the film Manny was still making up his mind. What he knew for sure was that he found a familiar comfort in watching the lives of others unfold before his eyes. It reminded him of home, and he was missing heaven's big-screen view more than ever.

There was still no word from Gabriel, but Manny had the sinking feeling his mission had ended in defeat. He had seen Chelsea looking over legal documents from Sawyer, and it didn't take an angel's view to know

259

what that meant. He had lost. And he wasn't the only one losing.

With one clean swipe of a light saber, Darth Vader cut off Luke's hand. Manny shrieked, clutching his wrist, which now seared with pain thanks to a vivid imagination.

Darth Vader's ominous mechanical breath always sent a chill down Manny's spine. "If only you knew the power of the Dark Side . . ." the evil lord growled at Luke Skywalker, his fist clenched as he threatened the vulnerable young Jedi. Then came the kicker. "I am your father."

"What? Nooooo!" Manny stood on his seat, his fists and popcorn flying. "Noooo!" Manny continued, now shouting in unison with Luke.

When Luke fell down the shaft to certain death, Manny was ready to walk out of the movie. But there was one more plot twist that kept him at his seat.

A flash of light, bigger and brighter than Manny had ever seen with human eyes. Standing before him like a ball of white-hot fire in an almost human form was the Archangel Michael. He was tall, though not as tall as Manny had imagined. They were nearly eye to eye, but then again, Manny was still standing on the seat of his chair.

Unsure if he should fall to his knees or stand at attention, Manny froze, hugging his supersize bucket of popcorn.

"Hi Manny," Michael said.

"You know my name?" Manny extended his popcorn bucket to Michael. If anyone deserved to be treated with the Golden Rule, it was the archangel.

"Of course I know your name," Michael said, waving off the bucket with a grin. "We're working on the same mission, remember?"

Manny's shoulders fell, popcorn spilling at his side. "I haven't heard from anyone in a while. Did the mission fail?"

"It only fails when we give up," Michael said. "And heaven never gives up."

Manny nodded, thankful for the reminder. "So where's Gabriel?"

"He's deep in the fight. But he needs your help. We all do."

"Me?" Manny asked, noting the intensity blazing in Michael's eyes.

"The forces of darkness are raging tonight, Manny. Get to the café as fast as you can. Chelsea needs you."

Manny swallowed his nerves (along with a few kernels that had gotten stuck in his teeth). "And when I get there?"

"You'll know what to do."

Manny ditched his popcorn bucket and darted down the aisle, the film's soundtrack building as he headed off to battle. By the time Manny reached the exit, his spirits were soaring. He paused in the doorway to offer Michael some parting words.

"May the Force be with you," he said, bowing his head.

"And also with you, Manny. And also with you."

CHAPTER 47

Chelsea turned off Hancock and Emily's night-light and slipped out of their bedroom. She stayed in the room with the kids until they were sleeping peacefully, cherishing one more night of serenity before she turned life as they knew it on its head. Hancock knew change was coming. But Emily? Would she rest as easy tomorrow?

Chelsea had begun to have nightmares soon after she learned of her own parents' divorce. Ominous shadows lurked in her dreams well into adulthood. As a child, she could almost sense them waiting for her to fall asleep. The thought of her own daughter being plagued with such terrors made her cringe. But it was soon replaced by a thought that troubled her even more. Would her children blame her the way she had blamed her father? How could they not? When it came down to it, the choice to split up the family was hers. These questions raced through her mind until they were lapped by one that had been running circles in her head all day.

How will I make it on my own?

Chelsea was finally ready to find out.

The router came to life with a zap that made her take a step back. In the pitch-black café, the glowing orb looked more spectacular than ever, its blue lights flashing like lightning bolts. They seemed to move in time with the crashes of thunder echoing through the night outside.

The movement of the trees bending and cracking behind the bay window in the sun-room was reflected on her laptop screen. She watched the cursor blink at the end of her eight simple words. With a burst of resolve, Chelsea struck the key. She watched as her question instantly appeared on the God Blog. If the past were any indicator, she would soon be hearing from the Almighty Answerer in the Sky.

Craaack! Thunder reverberated through the sunroom. The lamps flickered and faded, leaving Chelsea with the blue light of her laptop.

"You've got to be kidding me!" Chelsea exclaimed, staring at her screen.

She had lost her wireless connection to the God Blog. She closed the laptop, stood, and felt her way toward the door. She was nearly out of the room when she caught her first whiff of smoke.

Manny was out of breath. He had run ten full blocks, but there were still several more to go. How he missed his wings! For a brief moment he considered stopping to rest, until he recalled the archangel's words. *Heaven never gives up.*

Manny rounded the corner onto King William Street, his heart uttering silent prayers for Chelsea, Hancock, and Emily. When he spotted the Higher Grounds Café, he grasped the urgency of his task. Chelsea's home was engulfed in flames. Smoke billowed out of the shattered front door.

"Chelsea!" Manny called, sprinting toward the café. As he stepped onto the front porch, Hancock leaped through the broken glass opening, knocking Manny over.

"Hancock! Are you okay? Where's Emily and your mom?"

But Hancock was overtaken by a spasm of violent coughing. Seconds later, Manny received his answer as Sawyer emerged from the café, holding Emily in his arms.

"Chelsea . . ." Sawyer gasped for air, struggling to speak. "Can't find her upstairs . . ."

Manny needed no more answer than that. Seconds later he was racing through the smoky darkness in search of the person he was sworn to protect.

"Chelsea!" Manny called, but the only sound he heard was the blazing fire, angrily devouring the century-old house. He stepped toward the kitchen, his arms stretched out before him. Without his angel eyes he could see next to nothing. But Manny pressed on. Like Luke Skywalker boldly navigating the Death Star with nothing but the Force, Manny launched himself forward, trusting in something bigger than himself.

As he neared the café counter, an explosion of flame burst through the wall near the storage pantry. Manny ducked to avoid a downpour of fiery debris. From what he could see, the fire was emanating from the very place where Chelsea kept the precious router. He doubted this was a coincidence. Manny could only imagine what his unseen angelic compatriots were battling in this very space.

"Chelsea!" Manny called through the swinging door of the kitchen. No answer. And no sight of her either. Time was running out, and Manny couldn't afford to lose his wits. He closed his eyes to the world around him and listened. Though his angelic senses had been dulled by the clamor of the tangible world, Manny prayed he could still hear, still see something more.

God protect my daughters . . .

Give Chelsea eyes to see how much you love her . . .

The chorus of prayers, still resounding from decades past, every bit as potent as when they first were offered to heaven. And in this moment, they were louder to Manny than the destruction around him.

Bring healing to my family . . .

Lord, keep Chelsea safe . . .

Manny burst into the sunroom and found her lying on the floor. "Chelsea!" he called, but she was unconscious. As Manny knelt by her side, he could hear the ceiling above him giving way. He took strength from the echoes of prayers encircling them. Scooping Chelsea into his arms, he raced out of the sunroom, all the while dodging pieces of the crumbling ceiling.

Manny bolted through the café doors and into a line of firemen and paramedics. Even still, he refused to let her go. He kept running until he knew she was safe. Only then did his legs collapse beneath him. When the paramedics finally caught up to Manny, they were in awe that he had made it out alive, and with Chelsea no less. But then again, this wasn't Manny's first rescue mission.

CHAPTER 48

Chelsea's eyes stung as she opened them. Through a haze she saw Sara seated nearby, her head bowed in prayer, a singed photo album resting in her lap. When she opened her mouth to speak, she felt as though the contents of a fireplace had gathered in her throat.

"Sara," Chelsea whispered in a gravelly voice.

"Chelsea!" Sara rose to her sister's bedside, taking her hand, careful to avoid the IV. "How do you feel?"

"Awful, but alive," Chelsea said with a wry smile that lasted only a second. "Hancock and Emily?"

"They're okay. They're perfect." Sara poured Chelsea a small cup of ice water. "Sawyer has them. They've been staying at our place."

Chelsea took a sip of water, tears of relief

forming in her eyes. "Manny saved me last night."

Sara nodded, her own eyes brimming with emotion. "He did. But that was two nights ago. It's Sunday now. Easter."

"Was it Manny who got the kids out?"

"Actually, that was Sawyer."

"Sawyer?"

Sara nodded. "I don't know why he was there, but thank God he was. He's the one who called the fire department and pulled both Hancock and Emily from upstairs. But he couldn't find you, and the smoke had really gotten to him. Manny showed up right in time. He found you in Mom's old room, right near where the fire started."

"What caused it?"

"The storm. It hit just right and caused all that old wiring to short-circuit. The fire started, and once it did . . ." Sara shook her head, her voice quaking. "They said it's a miracle y'all made it out."

"So the café . . ."

"It's gone."

Chelsea swallowed hard. She knew it would take a while for that reality to set in. Still, she was grateful. Compared to the lives of her children and herself, the loss was small.

"Chelsea, there's one more thing," Sara

said, reaching for the photo album on her chair. "You had this when Manny found you. The nurses gave it to me with some of your things, so I've been looking through it. Just to remind myself of, well, how good God has been over the years."

Chelsea nodded, even if she did not fully agree.

"Well, I found this tucked in one of the pages." Sara pulled out a newspaper clipping from the *Tribune,* yellowed with age. Chelsea scanned the article, which detailed their fateful accident from her childhood.

"Look there," Sara said, rolling back the crinkled edges to give Chelsea a better view of the accompanying photograph, a rare artifact caught by an onlooker. "Do you see that?"

Chelsea studied the fuzzy photograph. Emerging from the fiery wreck was a man cradling an eleven-year-old Chelsea in his arms. This mysterious hero was Hispanic, around age thirty, and strikingly familiar.

"Call me crazy, but who does he look like to you?"

"It's . . . it's Manny," Chelsea said, her head shaking in disbelief.

"Exactly!" Sara exclaimed. "But how?"

Chelsea awoke this time to the sight of a

kindly nun dabbing her forehead with a damp cloth. "Are you all right, honey? You were mumbling in your sleep."

"Is it still Easter?" Chelsea whispered.

"It is indeed," she said, offering Chelsea the straw from a Styrofoam mug. "I'm Sister Margaret. I'll be looking after you this evening." Sister Margaret's smile was deep and sincere, as if etched into her face from years of loving care.

Chelsea drank deep, the cool liquid a comforting balm to her scorched throat. "Thank you."

"Anything else I can do for you?"

"Is there a chapel in the hospital?" Chelsea asked.

After assisting Chelsea into a fresh white hospital gown, Sister Margaret wheeled her through the double doors of a simple chapel. Chelsea continued down the center aisle, which extended the length of three oak pews, ending at an altar beneath a polished wooden crucifix.

"Shall I leave you for just a bit?" Sister Margaret asked.

With a nod from Chelsea, Sister Margaret locked the wheelchair in place and slipped out the door, leaving Chelsea alone in the silent sanctuary.

Chelsea stared at the cross, her mind

flooding with so many things she wanted to yell, ask, and scream. But amongst the torrent, eight simple words floated to the surface.

"How will I make it on my own?" Chelsea asked of the heavens through a stream of tears. Yet once again her question seemed meaningless, destined to remain unanswered, as if she had cast a message in a bottle into an infinite sea of stars.

A twinkle of light caught Chelsea's eye. She wiped her eyes and turned to see a familiar face in the pew beside her.

"Manny?"

"Hi, Chelsea," he answered.

Chelsea blinked as her eyes adjusted to a bright light. She was certain the face smiling back at her was indeed Manny, but something was different. He glowed, as if illuminated from the inside out. Chelsea didn't dare say aloud the thought crossing her mind. Instead, she formed her words carefully. "You're . . . not from around here, are you?"

Manny chuckled. "You've got that right."

"So you're —" She still couldn't say it.

"An angel," Manny said matter-of-factly. "Your guardian angel."

"Is this real life?" Chelsea glanced around the empty sanctuary, rubbing her forehead.

273

Her imagination was in crisis mode. The Manny she was looking at was anything but human. But that was impossible. An impossibility that offered answers to the questions she had been asking for months. Chelsea's steel trap of a mind had been sprung wide open.

"So the God Blog? That was you?"

"Oh no. I suggested the idea. But the answers? All him." Manny pointed to the heavens.

"And the people who brought the router, they were also —"

Manny nodded. "Just like me. But in better-looking disguises."

"And . . . the car accident?"

Manny nodded. "He sent me there too."

Chelsea held her forehead, struggling to put the pieces together.

"The question you were asking," Manny said.

"How will I make it on my own?" she offered.

"Chelsea, you won't ever have to make it on your own." Manny took her by the hand. "Let me show you."

CHAPTER 49

Chelsea was still sitting in the chapel. She knew this because she could still feel the rough hospital carpet beneath her feet and the cool metal of the wheelchair behind her knees. But her surroundings appeared to be the expansive Seattle home her family had lived in for three punishing years. The floor-to-ceiling windows of the white, airy living room showcased a rare sunny day, though even at its brightest, the Seattle sky seemed overcast to a Texas girl like Chelsea.

"Mom, Emily's trying to fly her dolls in my model planes!"

As soon as Chelsea heard Hancock's voice, she placed the day. The phone would be ringing any minute. The tired thread holding her life together would snap.

"Manny, I don't want to be here," Chelsea whispered.

But it was too late. She already was. An eerie chill went down Chelsea's spine as she watched herself enter the living room to answer the ringing telephone. It was like watching a stage play, and she was the lead. Too bad it was a tragedy.

The room seemed to be darkening by the second. As Chelsea peered into the shadows, she noticed faceless forms moving around the perimeter of the room, encroaching on their unknowing suspect. The nightmare that haunted her over the years had come to life before her eyes. Chelsea was thankful Manny still had her by the hand.

"Just wait," Manny whispered as Chelsea gripped his palm. "I want you to watch the windows."

Chelsea's eyes drifted to the windows, where the sun was overtaken by a beam of light that swelled and multiplied by the second. But these were no ordinary lights. At the white-hot center of each beam was a radiant figure unlike any Chelsea had ever seen. As these figures entered the room, their dynamic lights scattered the shadowy figures, forcing many into hiding. Only the darkest, boldest villains remained, encircling Chelsea's former self.

As the old Chelsea crumpled to the floor with the news of her husband's infidelity, a shock of light dropped down from above, dispelling the darkness around her. The radiant glow covered her like a cloak.

Even as a bystander to the scene, Chelsea sensed the wave of warmth rippling toward her, wrapping her in a healing embrace.

"Is that you?" Chelsea whispered to Manny.

"Oh no, Chelsea. That's him."

"He was there?"

"He's always been there. See?"

Chelsea followed Manny's gaze. Now she was looking at the steepled ceiling of the old wedding chapel in Alamo Heights. She saw herself making the long, lonely walk down the aisle. She knew this scene all too well. She had lived and relived this moment a million times. But this time it was different. Chelsea thought she had walked the aisle alone. She hadn't. She wore a veil of that same dazzling light, which enveloped her every move. God was with her.

For the first time, Chelsea experienced the memory of her wedding day unshadowed by a heavy cloud of shame. She noticed her mother, nodding her encouragement from the front pew. Sara smiled at the end of the aisle, in spite of the blue taffeta bridesmaid dress. Then her eyes landed on Sawyer, waiting at the altar, held together by a stiff tuxedo. She remembered his trembling smile, but his watery eyes reflected a deeper love than she recalled.

With Manny as her guide, Chelsea journeyed through memory after memory. Every moment of loneliness, abandonment, and heartache was revisited. Redeemed. From the discovery of her accidental pregnancy to the accident that nearly claimed her life, even Chelsea's darkest memories were illuminated by heaven's presence. A barrier had been broken. Beneath the hard, painful surface of her recollection were layers of healing truth. God had never left her side, not even for a moment.

"But why?" Chelsea asked as the last scene vanished from view. "Why me?"

"Because he loves you. In this moment. In every moment. He loved you before you uttered your first prayers with your mother on Easter morning. Even before you were born." Manny paused as a wave of emotion passed over him. "Would you like to see for yourself?" he asked, offering his hand to Chelsea one more time.

Chelsea clasped tight to Manny. As their palms touched, Chelsea's surroundings made their most dramatic transformation yet. To her left she saw an archway that led into an ancient city. To her right, about half a mile in the distance, she saw a hill.

"Where are we?" Chelsea asked. "Or

should I say, when are we?"

"You are on a path that leads out of Jerusalem to Golgotha. Over two thousand years ago."

As they drew closer to the hill, Chelsea noticed a trio of posts on its brow. Like props for a passion play, they loomed over the crowd, but the scene unfolding was brutally real.

The cloudless sky deepened to the color of a bruise and then to blackness. Chelsea could see only enough to make out the silhouetted figure of Christ on the cross, his arms in a V position. His chin rested against his chest and his hands were held by nails. He groaned, his breaths growing further and further apart as dark forces slithered around his chest, gripping his body like a boa constrictor.

Chelsea scanned the crowd for some glimmer of light, but all she saw was darkness. Then out of the black came a fearsome cry that silenced the clamoring crowd.

"My God, my God, why have you abandoned me?"

His language was foreign to Chelsea, but Manny had given her access to his eyes and ears, so she understood the words.

Chelsea watched in horror as Christ's head fell limp for several moments. Then he pressed himself up on the nails and cried out, pausing between each word: "It is finished!"

Bitter tears stung Chelsea's eyes. She couldn't bear another moment of the cruel struggle. "Why did you bring me here, Manny?"

"This is the loneliest point in history. The last moment of true abandonment. From here on, abandonment is nothing more than a myth. And loneliness? A choice."

As Manny spoke, their bleak surroundings melted away. Dark, heavy clouds shifted in the sky, revealing a brilliant morning sun that chased away the shadows. The hard rocky ground bloomed and flourished beneath her feet. Chelsea now stood in a bright garden. Vines worked their way up a stony wall. Flowers were lifting in the morning sun. The sky was brilliantly blue. On the other side of the garden, a large rock sealed the entrance to a tomb.

"There is no separation. There is no chasm between you and the heavens. There is no divider, no veil between you and God's love."

That's when Chelsea saw him. Jesus. Fully alive. His robe was a ray of sunshine, each thread radiant. His face shone like a full moon, the perfect reflection of his Father in heaven. The very sight of Jesus brought passersby to their knees. But for Chelsea, that moment came when she caught a glimpse of his eyes, like blazing stars. The same light that was present in her darkest hours was shining back at her.

"You wanted to know how you'll make it on your own?" Manny asked as the sights and sounds of the lush Jerusalem garden gave way to the sterile hospital chapel. "You'll never know. Because you never will be."

CHAPTER 50

Chelsea recalled the words of a familiar passage of Scripture, her Grandmother Sophia's favorite. "The house did not fall, because it had its foundations on the rock." As Chelsea explored the ruins of the Higher Grounds Café and its adjoining homestead, she imagined her grandmother would be smiling. To be sure, few of Chelsea's earthly belongings remained. Save for the stainless steel ovens, the metal speaker of the old record player, and the charred frame of the Queen Anne sofa upon which Lady Bird Johnson once sipped cappuccino, very little was even recognizable. But the walls, thick and heavy, the handiwork of masons from generations past, stood tall upon the café's stony foundation.

When the insurance adjuster arrived, he gave a curious whistle. "Special place you got here."

"Thanks for reminding me," Chelsea said.

"No, really, you don't come across these places much anymore."

"These places?"

"I'm sure you know," the man said, swinging his clipboard in a wide open semicircle, gesturing to their surroundings. "All this land once belonged to an old mission. It predates the Alamo."

"That's what my mother told me. And my grandmother before her."

"Yeah, but I 'spect it's more than that," he said, stomping the ground beneath them. "This structure could have been part of that original mission."

As the adjuster continued his survey, Chelsea wandered through the wreckage, recovering a few mementos along the way. That some of the items had survived the fire was nothing short of miraculous. A hand-carved rocking horse her parents had bought for her on a rare, happy vacation to Mexico. The needlepoint pillow her mother had stitched so many years ago. Chelsea read the phrase, *Living on coffee and a prayer.*

"Words to live by!" Bo shouted from the singed doorframe. "Thank God you all made it out alive."

"Thank God for Sawyer and Manny!" Chelsea added as her neighbor gripped her in a tight hug.

"How is Manny? I managed to see the rest of your family at the hospital, but I didn't get a chance to shake his hand."

"Manny is . . . great. He really is an angel," Chelsea said with a smile. "But I don't think we'll be seeing much of him for a while."

"Oh?"

"He was needed back home," Chelsea said, averting her eyes from Bo's. There was no simple explanation for Manny.

"Amazing how help comes just when you need it, huh?"

"It certainly is," Chelsea said.

"So what's the plan?"

"A lot of that depends on him," Chelsea said, gesturing to the adjuster. "I'd like to reopen the café. If I can afford it."

"I'd love to help any way I can. I know a thing or two about construction," Bo said with a wink. "Looks like there's some stuff here we could salvage."

As the adjuster finished his report, Chelsea and Bo rummaged through the wreckage of Chelsea's sunroom. Sadly, Bo's table looked more like half-burned firewood than, well, a table. Yet some items she still recognized. The face of Diana Ross on the cardboard cover of the Supremes' *Cream of the Crop,*

Paul McCartney's mop top on *A Hard Day's Night,* and most surprising of all, her mother's favorite album, *Put Your Dreams Away,* appeared untouched by the brutal flames. As Chelsea plucked the record from the ashes, she noticed something beneath, an inscription on the stone floor, buried by layers of wood and carpet but newly revealed by the devastating fire.

"Would you look at that!" Bo said.

Chelsea kicked away the debris to uncover the entire inscription, a sacred phrase no doubt chiseled into the very foundation of her home by the original inhabitants many centuries ago. *Casa de Oración.*

Chelsea translated it aloud. "House of Prayer."

In the weeks that followed, Chelsea was indeed living on coffee and a prayer. Tony and Sara had opened their home to her and the children, making for a very full house. They were serving as foster parents for Marcus Johnson, which brought the household to three adults and five kids, including the twins, who had just begun to crawl. The close quarters strengthened the family bond like never before. And with every memory made, Chelsea could see that her sister was growing more and more rooted to her humble home in Lavaca.

"I used to think the answer was moving my family to a better neighborhood," Sara told Chelsea as she pulled the For Sale sign from her yard. "Now I want my family to make this neighborhood better."

Sara was not the only one in the family to have experienced a change of heart. Hancock seemed to have aged several years since the fire. Everyone noticed. But it was Tony who pointed out that he was handling their loss with a maturity that did not come with time, but trust. Chelsea knew without a shadow of doubt that the same light she had seen in her life was residing within her son. When Hancock asked if he could spend a week with his dad in Austin, Chelsea consented, her mind at rest.

CHAPTER 51

Rest. Chelsea was growing accustomed to this new state of mind. When Sawyer's SUV pulled into the driveway a week later, she was not overwhelmed with the onslaught of what-ifs and remember whens. A surprising sensation settled over her. Gratitude.

"Thank you, Sawyer," Chelsea said, planting a kiss on Hancock's forehead before sending him inside to drop off his laundry. "I still don't know why you were there that night, but every day I wake up so thankful you were."

"I went there wondering if it was a mistake. Now I know it wasn't." Sawyer reached into the backseat of his car. "I have something for you," he said, pulling out a long white poster tube. He handed it to Chelsea through the window.

"What's this?"

"Hancock said you were still figuring out what to do with the house and the café. I did a little digging in the public records, and I was able to track down your grandmother's original plans for the Higher Grounds Café. Turns out she had a couple phases of construction in mind. Hope that's not too presumptuous. I just thought they might come in handy."

"Wow," Chelsea said. "That's so special. So thoughtful." She paused, taking in Sawyer's humble smile and blue eyes, glimmering with hope. She could not recall the last time she had looked at him without the fractured lens of a broken past. Could this be the first time? "How is the job hunt going? Any leads?"

"I actually just got an offer. A coaching position at a junior college. It's in St. Louis."

"Wow. St. Louis." Chelsea nodded through a surprising tinge of disappointment. "We'll have to come see you this summer."

"I hope you do." Sawyer sighed.

As he pulled out of the driveway, Chelsea considered the highs and lows of the last thirteen years. Her memories still remained, each and every one, intact and as present as ever. The pregnancy, the walk down the aisle, the betrayal. But their sting was gone, replaced with deeper truth. The road before her was open, but Chelsea didn't have to walk it alone.

Sawyer had driven two blocks when something caught his eye in the rearview mirror. Chelsea. She was jogging toward him, her arms waving. He hit the brakes and shifted into reverse, meeting her at the halfway point.

"What if I made you a better offer?" Chelsea said through winded breaths.

"Better offer?"

CHAPTER 52

With a few cups of coffee, Chelsea Chambers could change the world. She just knew it. As the clock ticked toward the opening hour of the new and improved Higher Grounds Café, Chelsea imagined all the life that would happen there in the years to come. Old friends would reunite. New friends would be made. Hopes and dreams, laughter and tears, they would all be shared over cups of coffee brewed with love and, more often than not, a prayer.

Chelsea had never felt more at home than she did in the newly remodeled café. The restored walls of the original mission and the refurbished phonograph in the sunroom celebrated the café's connection to the past, while the industrial cable lighting, aluminum chairs, and sleek tables added a boldly modern touch. Chelsea knew her Grandmother Sophia would be proud, and she hoped her customers would love the new look as much as she did.

"Here, boss, I have something for you," Katrina said, offering Chelsea a steaming latte. "I'm a little rusty, so my feather design turned into, well, wings, I guess." She looked over her art with a critical eye.

"Looks perfect to me," Chelsea said, thankful to have her star employee back on the job. She had missed Katrina's ever-changing hair color and mismatched style.

"Okay, we're ready for you!" Bo's voice carried down the hall.

"So, what do you think?" Sawyer stood beside Bo, draping his arm on his new neighbor's shoulder as Chelsea took in their handiwork.

"Beautiful!" she said, admiring the last of the custom furniture. "You must have been up all night!"

"Oh, you know . . . who needs sleep?" Bo quipped.

"Are you sure you're not an angel?" Either way, Chelsea was convinced her neighbor was heaven sent. With Bo's help she had managed to stretch the insurance money to cover the cost of the remodel and most of the remaining tax debt.

With the chiming of the clock, Chelsea paused to take a few calming breaths before opening for business. As she reached for the

Now Open sign, Sawyer's hands met hers.

"We got this," he said, hoping to calm her jittery nerves. It worked. Moments later, Mr. and Mrs. Chambers opened the doors of the Higher Grounds Café.

The morning rush was half the size Chelsea had seen in the busiest days of the God Blog. Otherwise, it was business as usual. With a few exceptions. Thanks to Faith Community Church, the tip jar had been replaced with a "gift jar." Tony's congregation had started a benevolence fund at the café, and they were spreading the word that anyone in the community could enjoy a cup of coffee or a bite to eat. On God's house.

Chelsea anticipated this would bring a new kind of customer to her café, and she was right. They gladly served two under-privileged teens, an elderly veteran, and a single mom with four kids. What she didn't expect was the generosity it would inspire in her usual patrons. By the end of the day, the gift jar was brimming with proof that kindness is contagious. Deb and her husband even promised to match the funds, dollar for dollar, for the first week.

Tony and his sidekick Marcus stopped by to grab hot chocolates and to fill a giant thermal container with enough coffee to serve fifty of their friends in the Lavaca neighborhood. Later on, the pair returned with Sara and the twins, and together they camped out in the sunroom, fielding questions from the occasional God Blog seeker with prayer, counsel, and, of course, a bit of humor.

"After all, God always answers knee mail," Tony loved to say.

Chelsea finally met Manny's sisters — the Sisters of Divine Providence. The nuns had housed Manny at the convent during his earthly assignment. As it turned out, Chelsea already knew one of them from her hospital stay. Sister Margaret and her fellow sisters thrilled at the sight of the *Casa de Oracion* inscription, which was now the focal point of the redesigned sunroom.

"What a fascinating discovery!" Sister Margaret exclaimed. "We will be sure to keep the café and your patrons in our daily prayers."

"Thank you, Sister. That means a lot," Chelsea said.

"Of course, dear," Sister Margaret said. "And did you find what you were looking for in the hospital chapel?"

Chelsea looked around the café. Hancock and Emily were snacking on cupcakes with Marcus. Sara and Tony were seated on the sofa, each bouncing a toddler on their knees as they chatted with Chelsea's patrons. And then there was Sawyer. He rounded the corner into the sunroom balancing four steaming mugs.

"No," Chelsea said thoughtfully. "But I found so much more."

"All right, the fancy designs are Katrina's doing," Sawyer said, handing a steaming mug to each of the sisters. "I made the cappuccino," he added, gesturing to the least impressive of the frothy creations.

"Oh my," Sister Margaret said as a pitiful layer of foam collapsed before her eyes.

Everyone laughed, no one harder than Sawyer.

"As you can see, it's my first day on the job. I just hope it's not my last," he added, placing an arm around Chelsea.

After tucking the kids into bed, Sawyer swept off the front porch while Chelsea stepped behind the counter to craft a pair of drinks. She ground a batch of perfectly roasted coffee beans, savoring the rich smell that permeated the air. She pulled the lever on her shiny new espresso machine, sending nearly boiling water through the fine powder. Smooth, frothy milk balanced the dark, bitter espresso shots she poured from two tiny porcelain shot glasses. Chelsea breathed deeply, savoring the complex aroma as she walked out to the front porch.

"How about a lightly caffeinated night-cap?" Chelsea said, handing a mug to Sawyer.

"Now that is a cappuccino!" he said, after a sip.

Chelsea relaxed into a comfy new rocking chair, and Sawyer settled into the one beside her. "Well, Chelsea Chambers, we have our work cut out for us."

"But we'll make it — together," Chelsea said, looking up at the stars. "And I have a feeling it's going to be good."

She reached out for Sawyer's hand and took a sip of the cappuccino. The truth was, it was already good.

CHAPTER 53

Samuel watched from a distance, his heart bursting, his eyes shining like a thousand stars. Heaven's view was good. Very good. The landscape below was brighter than it had been in decades. Spires of light burst through the velvet sky, pulsing with the prayers of everyday saints. Entire neighborhoods once clouded in darkness were glimmering with hope. And Chelsea? She was glowing from the inside out.

"Congratulations on a job well done. Your work as Manny was impressive," Gabriel said, settling in for the best seat in heaven. "I know it wasn't easy, but it was worth it, don't you think?"

"That'd be an understatement. I mean, look at them! Does it get any better?"

"Believe it or not, I think it does," Gabriel said with a smile. "You should have seen this story from heaven's view."

"I can only imagine! Still, I wouldn't trade

it for my time on earth."

"Really? I had something for you, but if that's how you feel . . . I don't know."

"What is it?" Samuel's curiosity was piqued. "A sword? A better disguise?"

"No, no. It's more like a movie."

"*Return of the Jedi*? 'Cause I never got to see that one."

"Even better than that. This one is especially for you. Courtesy of the best Storyteller I know."

Samuel's eyes widened.

"Sit back and enjoy the show. You've earned it," Gabriel said, giving Samuel a front-row seat to an expansive night sky. A moving image stretched across heaven's big screen. To Manny's surprise, he knew every single one of the stars by name. Unfurling before his eyes was Chelsea's story from the moment he ran into her front door. Only this time, from heaven's view.

Samuel laughed and cried through every twist and turn, both seen and unseen to the human eye. As Chelsea's guardian angel, Samuel knew he'd been cast in the role of a lifetime, and he couldn't wait to watch over her as she lived out the sequel.

DISCUSSION QUESTIONS

1. In the story, Samuel is Chelsea's guardian angel. Do you believe in the possibility of a guardian angel? If so, what do you picture your guardian angel doing to impact your life?
2. The angel Samuel walks the streets of San Antonio as Manny, a *Star Wars*–loving barista. Have you ever met someone you think is a heavenly angel? What made you think that?
3. Early in the book, Chelsea admits that faith doesn't come easily for her, "yet she found herself living by faith each and every day." What does it mean to live by faith? Why do you think Chelsea struggled with it so much?
4. Do you relate to Chelsea's struggle? What kinds of situations shake your faith?
5. Chelsea says that she has "the hardest time believing that the God of the universe watches over me and you. The idea that

he loves us individually. It sounds nice. But it also sounds like a fairy tale." Why is this so hard for many people to believe?

6. What part of God's love is hardest for you to believe? Why?

7. Tony uses an example of coffee in one of his sermons. The parts may not be individually good, but together, they make something good. God works in the same way, bringing all things together for good, as he says in Genesis 50:20. What examples do you see of this truth in your own life? Think about dark moments in your past that God redeemed for good.

8. 1 John 4:19 says, "We love Him because He first loved us." In what ways is that verse evidenced in this book?

9. When Chelsea's friend Deb shares about her reconciliation with her husband, she says that her husband is more forgiving of her than she is of herself. Have you ever felt that someone loved you when you couldn't love or forgive yourself?

10. At what point in your life have you felt utterly alone? Who or what helped you realize that God has never left your side?

11. With God's help, Chelsea is able to forgive Sawyer, and their relationship is reconciled. Do you have a relationship that needs God's help? What would it take

to begin the healing process?

12. If you had access to the God blog, what one question would you ask God? What do you think his answer would be? What do you hope his answer would be?

FROM MAX:
To Tom and Susan — celebrating
your love of story.

FROM ERIC:
To Mom and Dad, for raising me
in the circus so I never had to
run away from home.

FROM CANDACE:
To my parents, for always making time
to play make-believe.

ACKNOWLEDGMENTS

Heartfelt thanks to the exceptional Fiction team at Thomas Nelson, who love stories and love sharing them: Daisy Hutton, Ami McConnell, Katie Bond, Karli Jackson, Elizabeth Hudson, Kerri Potts, Jodi Hughes, Becky Monds, Amanda Bostic, Becky Philpott, Ansley Boatman, and Kristen Ingebretson. I'm grateful!

— Max Lucado

ABOUT THE AUTHOR

More than 120 million readers have found comfort in the writings of **Max Lucado.** He ministers at the Oak Hills Church in San Antonio, Texas, where he lives with his wife, Denalyn, and a sweet but misbehaving mutt, Andy.

The employees of Thorndike Press hope you have enjoyed this Large Print book. All our Thorndike, Wheeler, and Kennebec Large Print titles are designed for easy reading, and all our books are made to last. Other Thorndike Press Large Print books are available at your library, through selected bookstores, or directly from us.

For information about titles, please call:
(800) 223-1244

or visit our Web site at:
http://gale.cengage.com/thorndike

To share your comments, please write:
Publisher
Thorndike Press
10 Water St., Suite 310
Waterville, ME 04901